The Witching on the Wall

by

Constance Barker

Prologue

Wendy Robinson waited nervously by the back entrance to the hospital. The young woman was running late, and Wendy was going to end up late as well. Not that her current patient was in any danger of giving birth right away; she'd just gone into labor, and while Doctor Martin seemed sure the baby boy was on his way Wendy knew it would be hours still.

She glanced at her watch. Almost eleven pm. Where was she? Maybe she had changed her mind.

Almost as though that thought had summoned the girl, she appeared around the corner of the hospital, looking carefully around for Wendy or for something else. Wendy went to her, glancing around as well. What they were doing was technically above board—she had the paperwork prepared already—but somehow the young woman's nervousness was infectious.

"Are you sure about this?" Wendy asked when she got close. Pleasantries weren't necessary. They'd both been planning this for almost seven months. "Perhaps you can keep her."

The pretty young woman, just eighteen, gave a hesitant nod. "I can't do it. Not right now, not with… everything going on." She touched a gentle finger to the parcel in her arms, nudging aside a blanket that protected a tiny baby girl's face from the cool night air.

Wendy's breath caught as she saw the little thing. She was beautiful, just a few days old but born with a shock of bright red hair. Not from her mother, Wendy judged.

"And… the father?" Wendy asked carefully.

The young woman shook her head. "He doesn't know, and I'd like to keep it that way. I've read the law; we're not married. He doesn't have a say." She sounded fiercely committed to it. Technically, she was right. Wendy had overseen numerous adoptions under similar circumstances, though she never truly imagined she'd be taking on a child herself.

She was old, or at least she felt like it. In her forties now, the prospect of having her own child was distant and fraught with potential complications. She and Ryan had put it off, and put it off, and now they were simply past their prime. Without a child in their world, it seemed like there was less and less to keep them tied together like they had been twenty years ago, when they first married.

"The father may have to know one day," Wendy warned the girl. "These things… they have a way of coming to light. You know that?"

Hard faced, the girl looked down at the baby, close to tears. Her voice was tight when she spoke. "We'll cross that bridge when we come to it. Believe me, if it was an option now…" she sighed, shook her head sadly and looked up at Wendy. "But it's not."

"I understand," Wendy said. And she did. She'd been working with the Coven for which Coven Grove was secretly named for most of her life. She wouldn't have dared speak about it to the girl, though; even if she could have. But the geas she'd agreed to when she first took over for her own mother as the Coven's midwife would have prevented her from doing so. Still, the girl knew; that was enough.

"You've been such a friend to us," the girl said. "I know how badly you want a baby girl."

Of course she did. Even the young witches seemed to know everything about everyone. Wendy tried not to let it unnerve her. She should have been used to it by now. "Will she… you know…"

The young woman shook her head uncertainly. "There's no way to know yet. She's my first. So, there's a good chance of it. If so, you know who to contact. Though, honestly… I hope she can just grow up normal."

Wendy flinched at the word. Normal? Why would anyone want to be? It hurt her heart to see the girl so conflicted with her own nature. If that sort of conflict was common, that inner turmoil about who and what she was, then maybe it was better if the baby grew up a 'normal' little girl. "I'll watch over her," Wendy assured her. "It will be good for her to grow up with two parents… Ryan will be a wonderful father to her. I always thought he would." Even if he did work too much. But he was so good with children, especially little girls—they loved him, for some reason; maybe for the same reasons Wendy had loved him since grade school. He'd just always had that clever charm about him that drew people in close and winked at them.

"And you'll be a better mother than I could be," the girl said finally. She took a deep breath, and stilled a sob in her throat before she passed the bundle to Wendy's open arms.

It was heartbreaking to see the change in the young woman. She looked like she might snatch the child back. If she had, Wendy would have accepted it. She never would have imagined separating a child and its mother; not after she'd seen the joy of a new mother as many times asshe had—so many she'd lost count. At this point her career was simply a river of joy and gratitude and miracles. That a young witch would give up her baby was unthinkable, in fact; the Coven clung desperately to their daughters, the heirs to their ancient ways.

It occurred to Wendy that it could be dangerous, taking on this child. There had to be a good reason. But as she looked down into those startlingly aware green eyes, she decided then and there that whatever danger was involved, she would weather it. Instantly, she was madly in love. Maybe, she thought, it was witch's magic, ensnaring her mind to ensure her loyalty to the child. If so, she didn't mind. Her eyes brimmed with happy tears, and sad ones, and ones born of emotion too complex to fit into those tiny boxes.

She handed a pen and the papers to the girl. It was a closed adoption. The papers would be filed tomorrow, and locked away in some bureaucratic vault. No one would ever know unless she and the girl both agreed to let the secret out.

When the papers were signed, the girl stared at them

for a long moment before she passed them back to Wendy, tucked safely in their envelope again. She took a long, sad breath. "I trust you," she said.

"I know. It means more to me than you know."

"But… I do have to be sure."

Wendy nodded. Of course.

The young woman closed her eyes and concentrated. Her lips moved, and the wind seemed to rise in answer. The clouds thinned, and the stars shined, and their light seemed impossibly clear in the night air, lighting everything around her up with a silver gleam. The whispered words seemed to slip into Wendy's ears and travel down into her chest where they wound around her heart. They were a question, like one she'd given an answer to years and years ago.

Wendy didn't know much about witch's magic; her particular focus was only on ensuring they had their daughters safely and outside of the hospital. But she knew that the last geas she accepted was done by a woman much, much older than Wendy. That kind of talent and power in a woman so young still… it was impressive, she thought.

The young woman put a hand on Wendy's shoulder. "Do you accept the geas?"

Wendy didn't hesitate. "I do accept the geas," she pronounced. And just like that she felt it there, sinking into her, an unbreakable oath never to speak of the girl's true parentage. In a way it made her sad—every girl ought to know who her mother was. But, then again, Wendy was her mother now. And she would be the best mother she could possibly be.

She kissed the girl's cheeks, and they spent a moment admiring the baby again, together. "Oh," Wendy said, "I should have asked to begin with. Do you… have you named the baby?" Naming, for witches, was a sacred duty and one she didn't think she had it in her to take over from one of them.

There was no need, though. The young girl nodded resolutely. "Yes," she said. She smiled slightly. "Bailey. Her name is Bailey."

Chapter 1

The phone rang. It rang again, its birdlike ring-tone twittering away while Bailey Robinson watched it and weighed the pros and cons of answering it. But, in the end, she did have a job to do. She swiped Poppy's name and squeezed her eyes tightly closed as she pressed the phone to her ear.

"Hi, Poppy," She said, cheerfully, in hopes that it would somehow mitigate her inevitable ire. Poppy's resting state of mind was irritation, regardless of what was going on. Everybody in Coven Grove knew it, expected it, and did their best to avoid it if possible. Except Bailey. Bailey worked for the woman.

"Oh, you bothered to answer your phone today," Poppy sneered over the receiver. "That's just wonderful. I need you at the tour office as soon as possible, drop whatever you're doing."

"I can come in about an hour," Bailey said, eyeing the stack of library returns she'd promised to help her father put away. She was doing more and more of that lately.

"There are barely eight thousand people in this town and most of them are tourists," Poppy snapped. "And half the locals can't read. How busy could you possibly be, Bailey? Do you have any idea the stress I'm under right now?"

Bailey sighed, and plucked at a red curl that dangled over her forehead. Far as Poppy was concerned, she was the only person who even existed in a fifty mile radius. Maybe the whole world. "I understand, Poppy," she said. "What's going on? How can I help?"

"You can help by getting here," Poppy growled. "Martha Tells and Trevor Sullivan are coming in today."

Bailey blinked, and then stood up from the desk. "Today? I thought that was on Friday, I—"

"It was on Friday, but they've moved the production schedule up and if I make them wait they're going to pick some other rinky-dink backwoods nowhere and take their money with them so drop whatever you're doing over there and come help me make sure that doesn't happen." She'd gotten louder and louder as she went, and with the last of it Bailey held the phone away from her ear.

"Okay, Poppy," Bailey said calmly, trying to keep her boss on an even keel, which was a slim prospect, "I'll leave right away. We'll figure it out, okay?"

"I don't need a pep-talk, Bailey, I need you standing in my office!" Poppy hung up.

Bailey shuddered, put the phone down, and rubbed her forehead to massage out the tension that Poppy always put there. She'd go, and soon, but not before she took a moment to recover.

She sat back down, took a few deep, calming breaths just like her father always told her to do, and tried to clear her mind. Orderly thoughts, he sometimes said, or use to when he talked more, were the key to not losing one's mind entirely.

"I know that look," a clever male voice said. Bailey opened her eyes to see her best friend, Avery, standing between the Fiction and Periodical rows with an armful of books, his thin rimmed glasses slightly askew, his shaggy brown hair barely shy of a mess. He'd be the one taking up the slack for Bailey's sudden disappearance. "Poppy wants you?"

Bailey nodded. "You know that reporter I was telling you about? Trevor Sullivan? The one doing the piece on the Seven Caves with Martha? Well, Poppy says they've moved things up. They're coming today. Which just about throws all my plans for rest of the week off and of course has sent Poppy into a blind panic. I swear, I'm not entirely certain Poppy Winters even knows how to have a polite conversation."

Avery winced sympathetically. "Ouch. Well, if you were putting money in her pocket I bet she would. The tourist crowd thinks she's a doll." He pursed his lips at the stack of returns awaiting Bailey's attention. "Well I guess that means those are mine now, huh?"

"You could leave them for me to get them later," Bailey said, forcing a smile. "That'll be about two weeks from now, when this whole thing is over. Poppy's too cheap to hire a real assistant full time."

"Too cheap?" Avery wondered. "Didn't she just get back from Cancun or some place?"

"St. Maarten," Bailey corrected. "It was Vegas a few weeks before that. How she gets anything done over there, I can't fathom."

"Oh, I bet I can," Avery said as he set his small stack of books on a cart and came over to lean on Bailey's desk. "She doesn't. You do."

"Well, you got to put in your time," Bailey sighed. "Poppy hates the business. Probably she'd only sell it for a mint, but one of these days I'm determined to have her at least let me take it over."

"And give up some of that cash?" Avery laughed. "Try not to hold your breath, Bee."

Bailey shrugged. Avery was probably right. But the shop could be so much more than it was. Poppy put in the minimum amount of work and thought into how the tours ran, the souvenirs in the storefront, and cut all the corners she could find. It made her some money, and taking on a full time manager would probably cost some of that—but with Bailey in the driver's seat, she could double what was coming in. She knew it.

Bailey loved the Seven Caves. She knew just about everything there was to know about them, but she learned more all the time. They had an enchanting, mysterious quality about them, from the ancient writings and drawings on the walls to the series of fascinating events that had taken place in and around them. They were the cornerstone of Coven Grove's entire economy—the town itself had grown up around them over the last century and a half and it wasn't an exaggeration to say that the caves were the heart of the town. Without them, Coven Grove had nothing.

For a long time, she'd even considered leaving Coven Grove to become an archaeologist. She never had—it was more of an exciting fantasy than a real goal; she envisioned herself unearthing long lost artifacts or legends from their strange, black depths like Indiana Jones. But it was something she day dreamed about from time to time.

It was the whole reason she'd endured working with Poppy for the last two years. Poppy was self-centered, rude, didn't give two wits about the caves, and barely knew a thing about them that wasn't posted somewhere in her shop. Since Bailey had taken over the tours, the number of visitors had more than doubled from week to week, and was still growing. Probably because listening to Poppy gave everyone just as bad a headache as it did her.

She pulled a bottle of aspirin from the bottom right drawer of her desk, and spilled two into her hand. Best to prepare in advance.

"Got a headache?" Avery asked.

"Not yet," Bailey said around the two pills before she swallowed them and chased them with cold coffee from the mug she'd set down that morning. "But soon. Poppy sets my head pounding within about ten minutes, on a good day. Probably five, on a day like this."

"I think she does that to everyone," Avery agreed.

Bailey grinned. Sometimes it seemed like her and Avery shared one mind between them.

"Well, I better get headed out there," Bailey said. She glanced at the stacks of books on her desk. "Oh… do you mind? I can get them tonight if I need to—"

"I got them," Avery said easily. "Don't worry about it. I suspect I can make sense of your chaos."

"Oh, they're already organized," Bailey said seriously, pointing to the stacks as she went, "fiction, non-fiction, history, and each of those is broken down and ordered by their DD code, and arranged according to where they go in the stack so you start from the top and this end of the shelf and—"

"I was kidding, Bee," Avery giggled. He rolled his eyes in a good-natured kind of way, and shook his head. "Poppy would be lucky to have you running the tour business; you'd have that place running like fine German clockwork from day one."

"Well, I'd at least keep the books up," Bailey muttered. Accounting 'assistance' was one of her many chores at the tour office, usually after hours and unpaid as a 'favor' to Poppy that she never failed to ask for.

Bailey stood, prepared to leave now that she was armed with some aspirin and a better humor. As she did though, Avery spoke again. "Oh, and just as an aside, that reporter, Trevor something-or-another?"

"Sullivan," Bailey provided.

"Uh huh, that one," Avery said, smiling. "He came in early this morning when he got into town, picked up a few books about the Caves on his way through the town. Seemed pretty nice. Very handsome." He winked. "No ring, as far as I could tell."

Bailey wrinkled her nose. "Trevor Sullivan has been on TV since I was little," she said. "He's got to be almost twice my age, Ave."

"I'm just saying you may get to spend a little time with him and that you should be open minded. He was very charming. You could do worse. Especially around here." There was a note of genuine dissatisfaction in his voice.

Avery was cute as a button, in Bailey's opinion. And he was smart, and well-read; he loved the library the way Bailey loved the Caves. Bailey only helped out here because her father ran the place and desperately needed her help doing it. He had just turned seventy, and refused to retire. One day Avery would run the library himself, Bailey didn't doubt.

He also loved Coven Grove too much to move away, even though his own romantic prospects in this little town were slim at the best of times; non-existent more generally. Still, he insisted he wasn't lonely. "Long as I got you, Bee," Avery had said before, "I'm happy to live vicariously through you—so you need to find a man, and fast!"

"How about," Bailey said carefully, "I let you know how it goes, and you can read into it whatever you like, hon?"

"It'll do," Avery said wistfully. "You better get going, then. Poppy's probably having an apoplexy by now."

She grabbed her jacket and pulled it on. "Poppy was having an apoplexy when she called me," she said. "Actually, I think she just lives in a constant state of apoplexy."

"True that," Avery muttered as he started running a finger down the labels on the spines of Bailey's neatly organized stack. He pushed his spectacles up with one finger, brow already creasing with concentration on the task.

Bailey rounded the desk, exchanged hugs, and then rushed toward the door.

She stopped halfway there, and made the rest of the trip walking slowly backward. "Oh, also, tell Dad about the ATC folks being here early. He wanted to put together a piece for the paper about the visit."

"Will do," Avery assured her, not looking up. He might have sounded distracted, but Avery never forgot anything. If there was one person in this town more organized and reliable than Bailey, it was Avery.

In her rush to leave, Bailey nearly plowed right into her elderly father. She stopped just shy, startled. "Oh!

Hey, Dad!"

"Where you headed, Red?" Ryan Robinson asked, as he accepted Bailey's hug.

She pulled back, and grimaced. "The tour office. Avery took my stacks, but the ATC people got here early. Now Poppy's about to lose her mind."

"Oh," her father said archly, "well it must be Wednesday, then. Or Thursday. Or any day of the week. Wasn't she gone to someplace tropical and far away?"

"St. Maarten," Bailey confirmed. "She came back last week. If she'd listened to me then, the rescheduling wouldn't have mattered, but… you know how she is."

"Mm," he grunted. "Well, that's good to know. You'll see if you can get me in to see Martha and Trevor?"

Not that he needed the help. Trevor had been one of her father's proteges when he was still working full time for the paper, but had outgrown his shorts, according to Ryan, and skyrocketed to anchor status on the local news station on the strength of his looks and presence.

Expanding to host Martha's documentary about the Caves was an unexpected turn for him, and Ryan was eager to find out; though, it would never occur to him to write what he called a 'character assassination piece'. He was hoping that Trevor and Martha both were simply taking an interest in the home town again after years away.

"I'll let them know, Dad." She smiled, and pecked him

on the cheek. He didn't seem as excited about it as he would have, though.

She didn't need to ask if everything was okay. It wasn't. Ryan was Bailey's adoptive father. She'd always known, somehow, that she was adopted, but they hadn't actually told her until she was ten. Then, Ryan's wife Wendy, Bailey's adopted mother, was with them. She'd made the whole affair a story of a family made whole, instead of a little girl given up. If not for her, there was no telling how Bailey would have taken the news.

More than a mother, Wendy Robinson had been a pillar of Coven Grove, a midwife who, over the course of almost forty years, had helped about half the people of Coven Grove come into the world. When she'd passed two years ago, a hole had opened up in Bailey's heart that was still very raw.

Whatever her pain was like having lost a mother, it probably paled compared to how Ryan felt. He'd become a different person since then. He still had moments where he was his old self, but they were fewer and fewer, and Bailey worried about his health. What she'd do if she lost him, she didn't know. He was an anchor, a constant in her life, always full of worldly wisdom and kind words and fatherly love.

He loved Bailey fiercely; they'd gotten much closer since Wendy passed.

"Well," Bailey said, instead of dragging up their mutual pain again, "get those writing muscles warmed up. I'll let you know how it all goes today."

"Let's hope that Irish luck of yours holds up, Red," he said. "Be sure and tell Poppy I said hello as well."

Bailey let out a rueful chuckle. Ryan and Poppy had had a bit of a row last year when she'd been working Bailey nearly to death for next to nothing. She'd gotten a small raise shortly after, though it wasn't much. Now, Poppy got a special scowl every time she heard Bailey's father mentioned, and Ryan never failed to let it be known how he felt about her in public.

"I'll do that, Dad," she giggled. They hugged again, and Bailey left him, already almost twenty minutes late—based on Poppy's ridiculous expectation of 'right now'. It was going to be a positively delightful afternoon.

Chapter 2

Poppy Winters was typically as cool as her apt name implied. That was, unless she was talking to a paying visitor. Then, she was all smiles and warmth; a warm hearth fire for Coven Grove's tourists to gather around. The sort that played on a TV screen, but with all the appropriate decoration, at least.

Bailey, of course, wasn't a paying visitor. So as she sat across from Poppy in her office, Poppy's ornate but sparsely decorated desk between them. Bailey tried not to take her boss's shortness personally. There was no point, after all—it wasn't likely to change in the future.

"Glad you finally decided to show up," Poppy complained, digging through her purse for something. "I'm drowning here, you have no idea the kind of stress I'm under to keep this place afloat. Martha Tells is a nightmare of a human being, it's no wonder she hasn't had a paying gig in five years. She has no idea how to act professional."

Bailey kept her commentary to herself. "Well, I'm sure once she's gotten used to us she'll relax a little bit. So, how can I help? Point me in a direction and I'll take some of this off your plate."

"That would be nice for a change," Poppy grumbled. She produced a lipstick from her bag, opened it, sneered at the color and then chucked it into the waste basket. "I swear to God, someone is walking off with my lipstick." She glanced at Bailey as though it might be her. Bailey wasn't in the habit of wearing any make up, much less anything from Poppy's gaudy collection of eye-biting color palette.

In fairness, Bailey was still coming into the full measure of her maturity. At twenty, she didn't have to try very hard to look pretty; and she didn't. It seemed like a waste of time. Poppy, on the other hand, showed every one of her forty-five years, probably because she spent so many of them being angry about things. Mostly, Bailey felt bad for her. Not because she wasn't aging with as much grace as some of the other women Bailey knew, like her friend Chloe from the bakery, with her beautiful, mother-earth charm and infectious joy; but because it seemed like it must be difficult to live life so stressed out all the time. Poppy was incredibly fortunate, from Bailey's point of view. She just wished the older woman could see it.

Thinking of Chloe now made Bailey's stomach grumble in complaint. She hadn't eaten since breakfast. It didn't look like there was a meal in the very near future, either.

"I need you to go out to the caves and make sure everything is setup for the shoot tomorrow," Poppy said matter-of-factly. "All the equipment was supposed to have been delivered, and the tech crew says they're on it but they're a bunch of monkeys and I don't want them doing any damage to the wall paintings. Make sure they aren't crossing the ropes or leaving their trash around. They'll probably need help getting the right angles for the shots, just tell them what to do. And do it with a little spine, for goodness sake, not that cheery, chipper thing you pull with the tourists."

Bailey was making an honest checklist in her head. "Got it," she said.

"You might want to write some of that down, Bailey dear," Poppy muttered. "It's just the start."

For no other reason than to try and make Poppy comfortable, Bailey took a sticky note from the tall stack of them that Poppy never used, and a sleek silver and black pen from a canister of them that only Bailey ever used. None the less, Poppy seemed to note this and rolled her eyes.

Bailey noted down the first few of Poppy's expectations in her own shorthand, and then waited for the rest.

Poppy never really did much, but she somehow always managed to make it look like she was busy. She typed away on her computer, her face a mask of concentration over her standard-issue scowl while Bailey waited patiently with a polite smile on her lips.

"Check in with Martha, but for the love of all things holy don't be a sycophantic fan," Poppy finally said. "The last thing we want her to think is that we're too excited to have her here. We're not. ATC is doing her a favor.

"Do suck up to Trevor, though; he's a big deal, and a local that made headlines when he took up the anchor job at CBC. He'll make more doing this, and he's promised to mention my company so make sure he has good things to say." She drummed her freshly manicured nails on the desk, glanced down at them, and then looked at one of them up close and made a disgusted face. "And book me a manicure at Delilah's. Not with Cindy. What I wouldn't give for a decent manicure. This place is such a backwoods grunge-hole."

Bailey wanted to say that this 'grunge-hole' was the only reason Poppy was able to spend so much time on beaches and in casinos gambling away the money her father had left her when he left her this business. How Poppy had turned out like she did was anyone's guess. Bailey hadn't known Mr. Winters very long but he was a soft-spoken, intelligent, clever old man who loved the history of Coven Grove and the Seven Caves. He was wise, and always ready with a subtle joke or an anecdote about the Caves or some bit of Coven Grove's storied past. He was part of the reason that Bailey loved the Caves so much, though she'd always had a strange attraction to them, from the time she was small.

"I'll take care of all of that, Poppy," Bailey said, careful not to be too cheerful. "And, I promise to contain myself around Martha, somehow."

Poppy narrowed her eyes. "Don't get smart with me. Get going. Time is wasting, and it is literally money. While the documentary is shooting, we're not taking any tours and what ATC is paying me is barely more than what we'd make."

"Well, hopefully the documentary will bring in more

tourism later on, when it comes out, right?" Bailey suggested. "It's an investment."

"And now she gives business advice," Poppy sighed to the computer. "So many talents for a girl with only a high school education."

With a sigh that was hopefully too quiet for Poppy to hear, Bailey stood from her chair and tucked the list of her boss's demands into her jean pocket, where it would stay until she threw it away that evening.

"I'll let you know how things are going," she said to Poppy, who had thoroughly lost interest in the conversation and was busy with some inscrutable task on her computer. It wasn't the books, or very likely work related at all. Bailey did all of that.

She didn't bother to say good-bye. Instead she slipped quietly out, and made her way to the back of the building. There was a path there that led down to the Caves. She could have biked, but a walk sounded nice and while Poppy was worried that the tech crew would ruin the site, Bailey rather thought that since ATC produced scores of historic documentaries it was more likely they knew how to navigate an important archaeological artifact without destroying it.

The way there was green with the final push of Spring's up-welling of vitality, wildflowers and trees alike bright with life and color and the penetrating hopefulness of the oncoming summer. The din of honey bees busy at their work of making honey that would soon be collected and sold in the town's weekly marketplace mingled with the distant sound of waves crashing against the cliffs that housed the Seven Caves of Coven Grove.

She slowed, and let all of this wash over her, cleansing her of Poppy's negative energy. Maybe it was silly, but she always felt like being around Poppy left a kind of stain on her; a stickiness of the sort she'd immediately have washed off if it were on her hands and could be removed with soap and water. What her boss left her with though was something different. It was a lingering, scratchy presence in her mind that had to be washed off with something else. A change of mood, maybe.

Coven Grove's beauty did that for her, and she could almost feel Spring rising up from the earth and coursing through her with its gentle, green, vibrant energy. A rising tide that swelled around Bailey's spirits and left them shiny and clean and renewed, no trace of Poppy's sand-paper energy left behind.

Bailey paused, absently, and glanced back toward town.

About that same moment, her phone rang. She resumed her walk as she answered with a grin. "Hey, Pipes! What's up?"

Piper Spencer's strained voice came over the phone, weighty with whatever fresh new disaster her twelve month-old was engaging in now that he could toddle around of his own free will. "Riley, baby, don't pull on that. Don't—oh, hang on, Bails…" There was quiet scuffling in the background, and then Piper's gentle but put-upon voice as she extracted Riley from something, or something from Riley, one or the other. When she came back, Riley's giggling was audible, probably from where he was perched up on Piper's hip. "Minor explosion of poo," Piper sighed. "Just another day in the fabulous world of motherhood. Telling you, Bails, you don't know what you're missing."

Bailey giggled, but didn't comment. She knew exactly what she was missing. Piper had had her baby just a year after they'd graduated high school together; that just a year after she'd married her husband Gavin, who she'd been sweet on since they were in sixth grade. Bailey still remembered the first note that Gavin had written his crush those nine years ago, with it's little check boxes for 'yes' and 'no'. "Do you like me?" it had read, with a little PS at the bottom, "Just so you know, I like you." As though that hadn't been obvious by his writing the note in the first place.

Gavin was still, to this day, largely oblivious, and it frustrated Piper to no end, though she'd never say it. Gavin provided for them, but sometimes seemed to think that was the extent of what Piper needed from him. Worse than that, he tended to let his mother have a strong say in how the house was run, and how their baby boy was raised. It drove Piper to no end of madness having to deal with the domineering mother-in-law on an almost daily basis, but she bore it with strained grace.

Bailey knew all this, and sympathized, and wished she could fix it for them but… Piper only ever said things were fine as they were. She didn't want the help, at least not yet, so Bailey let it rest and kept her nose out of her friend's business. "I was thinking I might take Riley out a bit later," Piper said. "Maybe to the square? Let him run around in the playground, have some coffee and high calorie anything-with-sugar-on-it? Thought maybe he'd like to see Aunty Bails."

Bailey stopped, bit her lip, and quickly calculated the likely amount of time she was about to commit to the documentary crew. It didn't look promising.

"Oh, Pipes, I wish I could but… I've got this thing with the ATC people today, and of course Poppy's basically put it all on me and… I'm sorry, Pipes."

"Are they here already?" Pipes asked. She sounded hurt. "I thought they were coming Friday."

"They were," Bailey agreed. "They came early. I don't know why, but I guess Poppy was surprised, too, and you know how she gets when things go awry. Maybe later you two could come down and meet Martha, and Trevor?"

"That's okay, Bails," Piper said, distractedly as she probably changed Riley's diaper. It was confirmed a moment later when she made a gasping sound of disgust. "I don't know how he makes it all… I swear his diapers weigh as much as he does, it doesn't seem physically possible. Well, alright love." She grunted, Riley giggled, and finally Piper sighed. "I got my hands full. Call me later? We should hang out soon, me, you, and Avery. I need some girl time, badly."

"We will, Pipes, I promise." Bailey waited, wondering

if Piper would want to talk a bit more, maybe give her a hint as to what was going on.

But she just made a smooching sound into the receiver. "Love you, Bails, if you see Avery first tell him I said so, too."

"Love you, too, Pipes. Talk later."

Piper hung up, and Bailey stuffed her phone back in her pocket. There wasn't much farther to go now, and as she came around the bend she saw the scene below—crewmen crawling over the First Cave like ants, placing lights, and getting readings off of boxes, and pointing and scuttling hither and thither carrying equipment. From here, she couldn't hear them over the crashing waves that echoed through the caves and up into the town, so it all took place in pantomime.

Among the other worker-ants was an obvious Queen Ant. Even from here she could pick Martha Tells out from the crowd. For one, she was the only one in an elaborate dress; red-carpet ready to accept her award for a documentary that hadn't even started shooting yet. Or, maybe that was just how she always dressed. Another woman, shorter, with thick, black-rimmed glasses that were visible from a distance stood next to her with a clipboard, busily scribbling on it.

That made the man next to Martha, dressed in a gray suit, with a shock of red where his tie stood out against a white shirt, Trevor Sullivan himself, handsome even at a distance. As Bailey completed her journey, she decided that maybe the age difference wasn't that big a deal.

After all, he looked much younger; and he was far more handsome in person than on television.

"Hi there!" She waved to them as she entered the site.

Trevor saw her, raised his eyebrows, and then gave a friendly wave; he didn't know who she was.

Martha did, apparently, though. "Good Lord," She wailed. "At last someone's finally here! I thought you'd all forgotten about me. Find me a clean chair in all this mess, please, and a bottle of water, we're late!"

As Bailey did these things without question, her spirits faltered just a little bit. Somehow, she'd expected this would be an easy process; fun, even.

The more she got to know Martha, and her assistant Gloria—the short blond woman with the glasses—however, the more she realized that was not going to be the case at all.

Chapter 3

Martha Tells languished in the warm spring heat as though she were baking in a desert. Bailey had gotten her a bottle of water—a task which seemed more suited to her assistant, but Bailey was determined to make a good impression—and Martha had looked at it, made a long-suffering face and merely shrugged. "I suppose it will do." Gloria informed Bailey snidely that Martha preferred Ogo; some kind of obscure 'oxygen water' that Bailey had never heard of and was pretty sure they wouldn't find in Coven Grove.

Trevor was pleasant enough, but barely got a word in edgewise from the moment Bailey arrived. Almost as soon as Martha was occupied with her water, Gloria launched into an inquisition about the residents of Coven Grove; especially the women of Grovey Goodies, the bakery where Chloe worked. "Are they locals?" Gloria asked. "How long have they been in Coven Grove exactly?"

"Since I was little, at least," Bailey told her. "Does that matter…?"

"The doc is as much about the community around the caves as the caves themselves," Gloria explained. "These women"—she consulted a small notepad— "Chloe Minds, Frances Cold, and Aria Rogers; do they spend much time at the caves?"

"I... wouldn't know," Bailey answered, confused about how that had anything to do with the documentary. "They just run the bakery," she said flatly. "That's all. But, nobody spends more time here than Poppy Winters. Except maybe me."

"And, why do you spend so much time in the caves?" Gloria pressed, her pen poised over the pad.

"They're just interesting, is all," Bailey said, watching for Gloria to note something down. She didn't. "I mean, you've been inside by now, right? They're mysterious; a curiosity that sort of just doesn't make much sense."

"How's that?"

Bailey watched the woman's furtive eyes. She hadn't once done something assistant-like for Martha. In fact, she seemed more like a reporter than an assistant. Maybe Martha's role in the documentary was more involved than Bailey had thought? "Well look at them," Bailey said, "and look at Coven Grove. We're just a small town, there's nothing really special about this place other than the Caves, and the writing in them seems to range all over the place—Egyptian hieroglyphs, ancient Greek, Native American, caveman paintings; even some Sumerian. It's an odd assortment of cultures, and the oldest parts are over a thousand years old. It's got this anachronistic appeal, and you'd think it would get more attention but this is the first time anyone's bothered to cover it."

"Interesting," Gloria said, jotting things down. Bailey tried to peek over the edge of the little pad, but Gloria tilted it up a little bit as though to hide what she was writing down. "You know an awful lot about the Seven Caves," Gloria said. "You're sure there are just seven of them?"

Bailey frowned. "Well, I didn't name them. But yeah, I know about everything there is to know about them; I run the tours. It's my job."

"Of course, of course," Gloria muttered.

"I want a red carpet," Martha said, out of nowhere, suddenly surging to her feet. She spread her hands, rolling out the carpet in her mind perhaps, and pointed to the Caves. "From the entrance, all the way through to the last Cave. I want to walk down it throughout the feature as I reveal the truth about the writing on the cave walls."

Bailey glanced around, looking for some indication of who she was talking to. Most of the crew were out of hearing distance, and busy setting up lights and testing equipment.

Martha and Gloria both stared at Bailey expectantly. "I'm… not sure I can get that much carpet by tomorrow," Bailey said. "And the caves are all twisty; they don't run in a straight line. I'm not sure how you'd get a carpet all the way through it… I might be able to get it for the entrance, though."

"Oh, is there not a carpet store in town?" Gloria asked pleasantly, though it was a poisonous kind of politeness.

Bailey nodded slowly, keeping her calm, though she

desperately wished she'd brought something more for her headache; it was already coming back. "There is, of course; but they'd need almost half a mile of carpet to go through the whole network. It's just not practical."

"Practical!" Martha wailed. "Of course it isn't practical, that's not the point! This must be a magical, magnificent affair—it needs to make the right impression." She stretched the word out like maybe it was one that Bailey didn't know.

"I understand that," Bailey said, "but it's asking a lot. If you'd have let us known a few weeks ago—"

"If you can't see to Ms. Tells' requirements," Gloria said coolly, "then I'm sure we'll be able to find someone else who can. Of course, the fee will have to come out of what ACT is paying Ms. Winters for this. But I'm sure she won't mind, if it's to pay for a competent liaison."

Getting a whole mess of carpet on almost no notice was above and beyond what Bailey thought a 'liaison' ought to be responsible for, but she didn't want to tick Poppy off any more than she already was. She held her hands up in surrender. "I'll see what I can do."

"This girl is entirely ignorant," someone said; Bailey wasn't sure who. She glanced around, shocked that someone would say something so rude.

"She probably had no idea what the caves are really for."

"Martha needs to calm down. If these people won't

work with us, this is going to end badly."

"I need to question the women at the bakery, Martha seems preoccupied with them. I bet they have something to do with whatever her secret is."

"Can't believe I came back to this backwoods middle-of-nowhere nothing. It isn't fair. I hate those women for making me do this."

Bailey's head was pounding. Martha, Gloria, and Trevor were all staring at her as she glanced around, looking for whoever was talking, but it didn't seem to come from any particular direction. It felt like it was coming from inside, like having a song stuck in her head that she couldn't stop hearing no matter how hard she tried. "I'll get your carpet," she muttered, "give me a little time. I'm sure I can work something out."

"Well you'd better," Martha snapped. "Do you have any idea who I am?"

"I do," Bailey said. "And everyone is very excited to have you back for a little while." She doubted that was true, now that she'd met the woman. Poppy hadn't been wrong, she was a nightmare.

"Of course, they still think I'm famous. They probably hope I'll move back here and bring all my money with me. Hicks."

"Excuse me?" Bailey asked. She looked past Martha at a worker who was working the screws on a spot light. The woman didn't seem to hear Bailey, and Martha thought Bailey was speaking to her.

"I said," Martha repeated slowly, "I am tired of not being heard."

"Sorry," Bailey told her, a reflex to cover up the fact that she wasn't sure what Martha was talking about. "Just a bit of headache. I'll go see about your carpet. Try to relax a little, maybe see some of the town. I'm sure it's changed a lot since you were here last."

"I seriously doubt that," Martha muttered. "Nothing ever changes in this place. Not yet, anyway." "That'll be all," Gloria told Bailey as Martha turned away from them. She flicked her fingers, shooing Bailey off.

Bailey glanced at each of the three outsiders, smiling. "Alright. Well. I'll let you know what I dig up."

She turned and left, pressing fingers to her temples to rub out the tension that was crushing her skull like a vice, or possibly trying to push it apart from the inside; she couldn't tell.

She breathed in the spring air on the walk back up the path, again trying to focus on the positive. Martha and her people would only be here for a few days, and then they would leave, and the documentary would air and Coven Grove would start seeing a lot more people— hopefully the pleasant variety of curious tourists that she much preferred to people like Martha Tells and her awful assistant. Trevor, she hadn't formed much of an opinion of, but at least he didn't seem as abrasive as the other two.

Footsteps crunched up the path behind her. Bailey

turned at the sound of them. She felt somewhat better, at least.

"She's so pretty. Young, though, maybe eighteen? Nineteen? Legal."

Bailey frowned. No one else was around. "What did you say?" She asked Trevor as he approached.

Trevor smiled. "I said sorry about Martha. She's a handful, to be sure. She's got her reasons to be upset, but I don't think it has anything to do with you. Or even the carpet."

Bailey narrowed her eyes. It couldn't have been anyone else speaking. It certainly wasn't her. Maybe she'd been imagining it. There'd been a lot of that, though. Suddenly she found herself worried. People that heard voices like that were called 'crazy'. Or, more specifically, schizophrenic. Had her mother been schizophrenic? Was that the reason she gave her up? It made sense. Good Lord, she could have any number of predispositions and not know it.

"I'm sure you don't have to be worried," Trevor said, concerned and peering at Bailey's suddenly dire expression.

She schooled it, and rubbed her face with her hands. "It's alright. It's just been a long day already. I'm sure I can handle Ms. Tells' request, I'll just go to both of the carpeting shops in town and see what they can put together." She sighed. "Um, so what can I do for you?"

"Oh, nothing," Trevor said. "I just had to get away

from Martha and Gloria for a moment. I've been a little sluggish, and thought I'd go get some coffee and maybe something good to eat at the bakery. Grovey Goodies. You've been there?"

Bailey grinned. "I live there most mornings. Best bakery in town. Well, the only bakery in town, but I bet they stand up to the whole state."

"I bet they do," Trevor agreed. "I've been going back every day since I got here, can't stay away. Well, if you want, you could… join me for a cup? Before you chase down Martha's all-important red carpet."

She really did need to get on that carpet request if she had any hope of finding it… then again, she could always call ahead, and Grovey Goodies was on the way, and probably Chloe would have one of her special, experimental cupcakes waiting for Bailey to come and try out like she normally did. Plus, seeing the women at the bakery always had a calming effect on Bailey's spirits and she absolutely needed that if she was going to survive the next two weeks.

Not to mention, his forward comment notwithstanding, Trevor was very handsome.

"I suppose…" Bailey said, and then, more confidently, "You know what? Sure. Let's go. I could use a bite to eat anyway."

Trevor smiled at that, and the two of them completed the walk back up to the tour office and then into town together.

Chapter 4

Grovey Goodies was the highlight of Bailey's day more or less every day. It was in one of the oldest buildings in town, a beautiful dutch style cottage with yellow siding and calm blue shutters. The porch wrapped around the whole place, covered by low-swept eaves and dotted with bistro tables. As ever, locals were scattered across the porch, chit-chatting over pastries and drinks both hot and cold.

Inside, Chloe, Frances, and Aria bustled about the place mixing, baking, and tending to customers at the counter, helping them pick out which mouth-watering cupcake or pastry they wanted from the large glass covered cases that lined a long bar that separated the front of the place from the back half. As soon as Bailey and Trevor entered, they both took a deep breath at the same time, inhaling the scent of baked goods and coffee that permeated the place all hours of the day.

Chloe spotted Bailey when they entered, and clocked Trevor as well. She smiled, maybe a little stiffly, but then waved Bailey to the corner. She'd see to them personally.

They took an empty table in the corner, each taking a seat on the dark wood bench that fit snugly into the corner of the place. "I've been coming here since I was a little girl," Bailey said when they'd settled in. "My

Momma used to bring me here all the time. The ladies that run this place took it over when I was small...I guess Frances' mother owned it before? Or maybe Aria's, I can't remember."

"They must know you pretty well here," Trevor commented. "We didn't even have to wait in line. I guess hanging out with you comes with perks."

Bailey shrugged, grinning. "Maybe a few. I'm their unofficial taste-tester. Have been since I was eight. We live in town, just a few blocks away; Momma used to let me walk here on my own about then, so I'd come every day after school. Chloe there is kind of like the executive chef, I guess you'd say; at least for the cupcakes, which are what everyone comes here for. She's always coming up with new flavors, but I get to try them out before anyone else does."

"Wow," Trevor said, impressed. "Local librarian, tour guide, and taste-tester to Coven Grove's famous and only bakery and coffee house. You're a busy lady."

"You have no idea," Bailey groaned. She heard something, distantly, and her head pounded once. She rubbed her forehead, and glanced around the place. There was a low level din of murmuring in the bakery, but it seemed to have an extra layer to it, a quiet cacophony of whispers that grew louder when she turned her attention to them. She cleared her throat, and tried to focus on Trevor. "So familiar. I wonder where I know her from. A long time ago."

"Who me?" Bailey asked.

"Pardon?" Trevor replied, his eyebrows raised.

"Oh, I thought you said… never mind." She waved the confusion off. "I'm a little frazzled today." Or possibly losing her mind. The jury was still out.

"You look really familiar," Trevor said, however, and Bailey stared at him when he did. Hadn't he just said that?

"You might not recognize me," Bailey said, ignoring for now Trevor's odd behavior. "But my father is Ryan Robinson."

Trevor's eyes widened. "Oh. Of course! How could I have forgotten that? Little Bailey Robinson! Geeze, I should have remembered that mass of red hair." He laughed. "Well, the last time I saw you you were… what, five years old maybe? When I first started working with your dad. You've grown up, that's for sure."

Bailey smiled self-consciously at the way he said it. She was about to say something, she wasn't sure what, when Chloe approached their table.

Chloe was a pretty woman, with long, thick auburn hair and bright green eyes. She was about Bailey's height and like the other two women she was a couple of years from forty but still looked like she could pass for twenty five. Where Frances had streaks of gray creeping into her red hair, and Aria had fine lines slowly spreading from the corners of her eyes, Chloe's face was smooth, her hair unmarred by time. Maybe because

Frances and Aria were sometimes a bit dour, while Bailey had not once seen Chloe without a pleasant smile on her face.

"Perfect timing," Chloe said as she came by. "For you, Mr. Sullivan." She said his name with bit of formality as she set down a drink in tall mug with a swirl of cocoa-dusted whipped cream on top, and a chocolate cupcake with rich, dark frosting on top. "Your usual, sir."

"Oh, thanks," Trevor said. "I didn't realize you all were paying attention! Gosh, I already feel like I'm back home."

"We notice everything," Chloe said smartly. She turned a brighter smile on Bailey, and set down a darker cupcake topped with a pale yellow frosting. "And for you, my dear. Tell me what you think—this one is a dutch chocolate base, with just a hint of paprika and orange zest, and the frosting is a lemon cream. Just something I whipped up special for you this morning."

"Thanks, Chloe!" Bailey chirped as her mouth watered with anticipation. Sometimes the things that Chloe came up with didn't seem to make any sense, but not once had she made something Bailey didn't like; though perhaps that was because Bailey was used to odd flavors now. How Chloe kept coming up with new ones was a mystery Bailey had never solved.

"I've got you a hot chocolate on the machine," Chloe said. "Just wanted to get this out to you straight away." She winked, and left to get it. On her way, she passed Frances, paused, and then moved on. Frances, a severe, gaunt featured woman with eyes that were dark but still somehow warm—at least when they were turned on Bailey—gave Bailey and Trevor a long look. Finally she winked at Bailey, and turned back to her oven to pull out fresh turnovers.

"So, how is your father?" Trevor asked. "I looked for him at the library, but he wasn't there. The folks at the paper told me he still writes; I would have thought he'd be retired by now."

"He was going to," Bailey said. "Just before Momma passed. Then, I guess he just needed something to do, so, he kept working."

Trevor paused, setting his drink down slowly. "Wendy passed?" He seemed shocked by the news. "When?"

"Oh, almost two years ago now." Bailey said, wincing. She supposed that Trevor and her father had been out of touch. Then again, Ryan Robinson wasn't often inclined to reach out to his friends or family for any kind of support. If you wanted to know what was happening with him, you had to dig.

"I'm so sorry to hear that, Bailey," Trevor said earnestly. "I knew Wendy a little bit; mostly Ryan and I worked at the paper, but… she was a good woman."

"I couldn't have asked for a better Momma," Bailey agreed. "She took me in when I was a baby, you know. Her and Dad both, and they weren't young when they did it."

"You were adopted?" Trevor asked.

Bailey nodded. The sting of it was there, of course, but it had dulled long ago. "They're the only parents I've ever known, of course. I used to feel bad, like my real parents had given me away; but later on it was more like Wendy and Ryan had chosen me, you know?"

"I get that," Trevor said. He sipped his coffee, and licked the bit of whipped cream it left behind on his lip. Bailey's eyes scrunched up with amusement. Chloe returned with a steaming mug of hot chocolate. Coffee was good, of course, but nothing beat Chloe's hot chocolate; she sprinkled shaved dark chocolate into the drink itself, and peppered the whipped cream top with a mix of cinnamon and just a hint of black pepper. It was a custom combination that had always made Bailey feel like she was special. If she'd had any skill at baking— she didn't, she could burn a pop-tart—she sometimes thought it would be fun to work at the bakery with the ladies.

"So how are you two getting on?" Chloe asked, eyeing them both, her hands on her hips behind her batter-dusted apron.

"Just fine, Chloe," Bailey said. "We're just talking." Having the three ladies looking after her did make the hole that Wendy had left behind when she passed seem a bit less painful; Chloe especially had become a sort of second mom, or at least a watchful older sister, in the last couple of years. Her suspicion regarding this handsome older man was obvious. She didn't bother to hide it from either Bailey or Trevor.

"Bailey's assisting us with the documentary at the

Caves," Trevor explained. "I'm giving her a bit of the low-down on working with Martha Tells."

"Martha," Chloe sighed. "She's a piece of work." She relaxed somewhat. "I knew her before she was famous, but you'd think she always thought she was."

"Less so now," Trevor muttered.

Chloe pursed her lips, and then glanced back at the counter. "Well, I've got customers to tend. You two be good."

When she left, Trevor let out a slow breathe. "I wouldn't want to make Chloe angry," he said. "I remember her from school. She wasn't quite so... forceful then."

Bailey giggled. "Well, you best watch what you say to me, then. Chloe, Frances, and Aria are all pretty protective of me. Especially now."

"I'm glad you have them," Trevor said quietly. "It's good to have a big family, a tight community. One of the things I always missed about Coven Grove, actually."

"That so?" Bailey bit into her tester cupcake. Her eyes lit up when she did. "Mm, this ith really good," she murmured around the mouthful, covering her mouth with one hand as she did.

Trevor chuckled, and went on. "Yes. I moved to Stinton, where both CBC and ATC are based. Same building, actually, just different floors. Oh, you got a little something…" He reached out, and swiped a bit of frosting off of Bailey's cheek. He looked for a moment like he might put it in his mouth, but then wiped it on a napkin instead.

Still, the little gesture gave Bailey a brief flutter. Well, what they said about him was all true, wasn't it? Quite the flirt indeed. She pretended it hadn't happened. "Well, I should go see about this carpet before it gets too late," she said. She popped the rest of the cupcake in her mouth, savoring the once-in-a-lifetime taste of it. Chloe rarely put these experimental varieties on the menu; for all Bailey knew she made them just for her.

"I wouldn't bother," Trevor said. "Honestly, Martha's so desperate for the spotlight, she'd do the documentary barefoot in a burlap sack."

Bailey burst out laughing, and then covered her mouth to keep from spitting out cupcake. The image of Martha Tells in a burlap sack, red-faced and raging but pointing at the cave paintings while she gabbed on about whatever she thought she knew about them was just too amusing.

Trevor laughed with her, and the three ladies behind the counter, as well as several patrons, gave them curious looks. "It's true, though," Trevor said as they calmed down again. "The reality is, Martha is done. She has been for a while. The only reason the studio took her up on the proposal to do the piece is that she's broke. She hasn't had work since she was here in the Grove, honestly, and she's barely making anything for this. It's all about exposure for her. She's got a lot of bark, don't get me wrong, but she's got no teeth to bite with anymore. She's convinced this place is going to change all that, but I'm not so sure yet."

"Why would she think that?" Bailey asked. That Martha had achieved any fame at all before leaving Coven Grove was a miracle in itself; doing it twice seemed unlikely, regardless of what she planned to reveal about the caves. Not unless she was a secret archaeologist looking to get a paper published and that wasn't the kind of fame Bailey thought would appeal to a woman like Martha.

"My guess?" Trevor said. "She's desperate and a little delusional. Grasping at straws, trying to find something that can dig her out of this hole she's in."

"A little old for her, isn't he?"

Bailey blinked, and glanced over her shoulder. Not that gossip didn't happen in Coven Grove, but it wasn't usually so overt and in the open like that; the people here were polite in public, at least. No one seemed to be looking at them, though. That headache again… maybe she should see if Chloe had something for it behind the counter. "You alright?" Trevor asked. He was getting to be genuinely concerned.

The din of whispers in Bailey's head was getting louder. She probably ought to go, and maybe even make an appointment with someone to get checked out. She tried not to look as worried as she really felt. "I'm okay," she told Trevor. "Just feeling the time. I'm going to go at least check on the carpet. After all, if I can make the whole thing more to Martha's liking then at the very least she might be in a better mood—and that's good for everyone, right?"

"You may have a point there," Trevor admitted. "Alright. Well, I've got some writing to get done, and some preparations with Martha and her assistant, so… I guess I'll let you go. I'll see you a bit later, I'm sure."

"Definitely," Bailey agreed. "Um… thanks for bringing me here. I needed it. It was… nice."

"Likewise," Trevor said, his eyes crinkled with his smile. Boy, but he had some white, straight teeth. No wonder he did so well on TV.

"Alright," Bailey said as she stood. "Well… then I'll see you later."

"Will do," Trevor said, still smiling.

Bailey left, breaking off the long good-bye before they ended up here all day. She waved to Chloe, Frances, and Aria as she did, and all three ladies chimed good-bye's and come-back-soon's as Bailey pushed through the door to the porch, and made her way to the library to get her car and check on the possibility of Martha's red carpet.

Maybe the whole affair wouldn't be all that bad after all. Except, all the way to the first carpet shop, Bailey heard those distant whispers and tried desperately to ignore them, to ground herself in her senses; but if she really was starting to lose her mind, could she even trust them?

Chapter 5

The feel of the steering wheel under her fingers. The smell of her car. The breeze on her face with the window down. The music playing through the radio, something popular that she'd heard so many times she could sing along without really thinking about it. The taste of the salt in the air.

Focusing on these things to the exclusion of all else helped calm the whispering down until it was a distant, far away background noise—like the ever present sound of the ocean throughout town, so constant and far away that no one even really heard it anymore unless they tried to. So, that was good.

On the other hand, she passed the Rigby's Carpeting Depot twice before she managed to get parked in front of it.

Her visit was urgent, but polite, and she managed to secure a little under half of what Martha wanted; though whether it would be ready by tomorrow was a question of how much ACT would be willing to spend.

Hitch-Morgan's Flooring didn't think they could make up the other half, but Bailey told them to just get whatever they could together and she would make do. Maybe, she figured, they could just re-lay the carpeting from the entrance of the Caves into the back. Surely they could just edit it to look continuous, right?

That done, and Bailey's mind thoroughly occupied with the logistics of the whole affair, she barely heard the whispers in the back of her mind any more. Maybe it was just the stress. Crazy people were crazy all the time, right? Maybe it was a little early to call in the shrink.

She pulled into the tour office to give Poppy the updates on what was happening, but found the place empty. Maybe she was at the Caves, speaking with Martha. It was getting on into the afternoon.

So Bailey left her car there and walked back down the long path to the Caves, trying to calculate the best way to cut the carpets so they could keep a lead on the camera crew. That seemed like the best way to do it, and if they had maybe four or five sections they could stay out of sight around the next bend; plus one straight ream of carpet wasn't going to do it—the Caves had odd angles and turns that would bunch it up and she suspected Martha wanted it to be smoothed out, the way it was for big events like the Oscars or other celebrity award ceremonies.

She rolled her eyes a little at that thought. What exactly did Martha think this event was going to do for her? ACT did some well-done documentaries, there was no doubt about that; Bailey loved them, but then she was a bit of a self-admitted nerd when it came to history and the odd, interesting bits of archaeological lore that ACT was particularly focused on. Ten million viewers, this documentary was not likely to have.

And the whole idea of 'revealing the secret of the Seven Caves' seemed almost silly. What could Martha possibly know that Bailey didn't? Not to toot her own horn, but Bailey figured she knew about all there was to know about the Caves.

When she arrived, the lights were set up, along with tripods and tracks for cameras, and there were locked boxes of equipment strewn about. Not even a guard was there to watch over all of it—not that one was really needed. Coven Grove did have a sheriff, but at this point Sheriff Tim Larson would probably hold the office until he retired or died, and it was practically an honorary title in any case. The crime rate in town was more of a footnote than an actual number. Probably something like 'too small to calculate'. Other than the occasional teenage vandals or a drunk driver—both still rare—Coven Grove just didn't have crime. There'd have been no way to get away with it. Everyone knew everyone else.

Well, she had measurements to make anyway. She'd brought a tape measure with her, so she wandered into the entrance to the Caves.

Every time she came here, she felt the same sense of familiar comfort. Being in the Caves felt as natural as being in her own home, and had that same sense of welcoming warmth and brightness even though the caves themselves were dim, lit only by the occasional shaft of light filtering down through holes in the cave ceiling.

They were entirely natural caves, though the floor was worn from centuries of feet walking over them and in places had been smoothed out a little bit in the last two hundred years. Like any natural cave, the canvas upon which the various paintings and writing had been authored was uneven; but whoever had laid it all out in the first place seemed to have taken care to use that unevenness rather than trying to compensate for it. So the wide sections of murals had a certain quality of three dimensional intelligence to them.

The cave paintings were a marvel of cultural cross-pollination. Some ancient explorer, she imagined, had probably been responsible for them, or a whole slew of them. Around ancient pictures of animals and figures of people, drawn in curling, winding sequences that put her in mind of Native American paintings she'd seen pictures of from elsewhere in the US, were letters in Greek, Arabic, Egyptian hieroglyphs, Norse runes—not Germanic; Bailey had taken an interest in them and learned the differences when she was only thirteen—and even long, winding lines of Ogham script that was historically reserved for marking on long branches but apparently had been transcribed here.

It was like a travel journal, she'd often thought. She dared not touch them, but she trailed her fingers around them, fascinated as ever and desperately curious about what they meant. Maybe Martha really did know. If she did, that alone made it worth dealing with her.

The most interesting thing about the odd collection of scripts and letters was that they didn't actually translate. They were like gibberish. To Bailey, this was evidence that the author hadn't actually spoken these languages; that maybe they had simply seen bits and pieces, copied letters down, and then decorated with them. When she was just turning twelve, she'd copied down every line and letter and worked tirelessly at the library digging through books on languages and symbols, trying to piece out what they'd meant.

She and Avery had done it together, imagining themselves intrepid junior archaeologists on the verge of a great discovery—the sort that would launch them into world fame. "Twelve Year-Old Genius Researchers Discover Meaning of Ancient Cave Paintings," the headline would have said. "World in Awe."

She smiled, remembering those long afternoons after school spent shoulder to shoulder, arguing about the letters, and running back and forth to the Caves to compare notes and pose their child-like hypotheses. Bailey had supposed, at one time, that they were actually magic spells, preserved here by ancient wizards or shamans who had traveled the world on the wind collecting the wisdom of dozens of cultures and concentrating it in this one place. In fact, she'd believed it so strongly that she and Avery got into screaming matches about who was right: her, with her ancient sorcerer theory, or Avery with his hypothesis that it was just mimicry.

Eventually she'd grown out of the belief that there was anything magical about the paintings than what was inherent to the place itself—which was to say, only it's mysterious nature. Avery's theory made more sense after they'd failed to translate a single line. On the other hand, both of them had learned a great deal about these ancient languages. She'd aced Latin in high school without working up a sweat.

In particular, her favorite painting was in the fifth Cave. Each of the seven Caves was defined by an apparent theme, and by the narrow passages that connected the wider caverns. The fifth cave's wall was one of the most bare, but it had the most complex art. It was unmistakably a woman, almost eight feet tall, her arms spread wide and angled slightly down as though to embrace the observer. The mounds of the cave wall served to give the impression that her arms were in fact reaching out from the wall, and the curvature of the whole mural was such that no matter where in the cavern you were, her simple, expressionless eyes seemed to follow you.

Except, Bailey had never really felt that her face was exactly expressionless. The artist had not given her a mouth, and only a spiraling mix of letters for eyes, two of them, each with different script, and yet she somehow seemed always to be smiling in Bailey's opinion. She couldn't have said why she thought so, other than this is what she felt when she looked at it. Perhaps that was the point—this was all the work of some early abstractionist who's goal was to make you feel the work, rather than just look at it. Whoever it was had been centuries ahead of their time.

Bailey watched the ancient goddess, enchanted by the whorls of fine lettering that made up her eyes. Above her head was a tribal depiction of the Sun, along with a star that she had long ago decided was meant to be Venus in the morning sky. There were several of these throughout the caves, though not all of them were as obvious—constellations and recreations of the heavens were a typical theme in many cave paintings the world over. Mankind had, Bailey imagined, always been fascinated by the regularity of those pinpricks of light in the heavens.

She shook off her fascination. She could gaze at the paintings and swim in the comfort the caves gave her any time she wanted. Now, she was at work and had a job to do. One that she'd hear no end of grief about if she was slow to complete it. She sighed, and got to work measuring and noting down the numbers and adjusting her mental calculations. They'd need at least seven different sections of the carpet, but two of the caves had roughly the same dimensions so maybe only five would be required.

She proceeded through the sixth cave, confirmed her suspicion of what was needed, and then walked toward the threshold of the seventh and final cave.

Something stopped her. The whispers in her head were gone now, driven off perhaps by the isolation of the caves, influenced by the near total silence of the place and calmed by the dull white noise of the ocean echoing through the place that had the strange effect of dampening all other noise entirely. Somehow, though, the lack of those whispers made her feel suddenly very alone and very small. The caves seemed to close in around her.

Bailey was not claustrophobic, and had never feared being in the caves. Now, though, she had a horrible, creeping feeling in her spine, as though something was watching her. It didn't feel exactly malevolent, whatever it was—her own stress, very likely, manifested in the dimness of the caves—but it felt... what was it?

Like a warning, she realized. Go no further, it seemed to urge her. Turn around, leave. The feeling started as merely a fleeting instinct, but as she pushed through the narrow passage it became more and more insistent, until she couldn't stop her own mind from chanting at her, "Go back, go back, go back..."

It was unnerving, and her hands trembled against the cave wall as she guided herself through the unlit tunnel, following the illumination of some stage lighting that was tuned down to almost nothing ahead. Her shoe brushed an orange extension cord on the ground, and she nearly jumped at the sudden instinct that it was some brightly colored serpent before her eyes focused on it properly.

She sighed. The tiny burst of adrenaline seemed to

have cleared her mind a bit and she laughed at herself a little, which helped even more. One more cave to go, and she'd run back to the carpet shop to give them the specs.

The final cave was undoubtedly of a lunar theme. The moon in its various phases, broken down into sevenths from the full moon to the new in a great circle that spanned the full width of the cave's perimeter near the ceiling—but with one missing spot, as though the artist had meant to divine the upper wall into eighths but had, perhaps, never finished the work. It was a gap that made the moon paintings, each connected and encircled by letters and swirling lines, look like a circlet of white seen from inside some king or queen's skull. Where the missing phase of the moon was, if that's what was meant to have been there in the first place, there was one of the most fascinating paintings in the whole system. One that made no sense, other than perhaps as someone's fancy.

It was, seemingly, a door. It arched gracefully up, and was on one of the flattest planes on the walls. The lines of it were made up entirely of letters and figures, drawn so tiny that without good light and a magnifying glass it was impossible to parse them out. It must have taken ages to finish with only the tools of whatever ancient artist had undertaken it. She gazed at the door, and then sighed when she saw a crumpled pile of something at the base of it. A dress?

She moved toward it to clean up the mess and then froze, her blood chilling as she saw it more clearly.

It was a dress; but there was still someone in it.

It was Martha Tells, and she was very clearly, very messily, deceased.

Bailey screamed.

Chapter 6

The Sheriff's department, an ambulance, and the local paper all arrived within half an hour of Bailey's call. She barely remembered making it. After her blind dash back to the entrance of the Caves, she had dialed 911, and then Avery, who had called her father, and the two of them had arrived on the heels of the Sheriff's department.

Now, a smattering of locals arrived as well, gathered outside the police tape, watching and murmuring among themselves while Bailey answered a deputy's questions as clearly as she could, barely holding herself together.

"She was there when I got to the last cave," Bailey was saying to the middle aged Deputy, Dylan Harper, whom she'd known her entire life like everyone else in town. "I didn't realize at first… it's dark back there, just a little light from the lamps the TV crew set up. I thought at first it was… well, that doesn't matter, I guess. When I got up close I could see it was her and that she was… she was…"

"It's alright, Ms. Robinson," Deputy Harper said. He'd never called Bailey 'Ms. Robinson' before. It made Bailey feel like a suspect.

Which, of course, she would have to be at least for now.

The next question confirmed it for her. "If you can recall," Dylan said gently, "where were you before this?"

"I went to Rigby's and Hitch-Morgan," she said confidently. "I was supposed to arrange carpeting for the caves while Martha and Trevor did the documentary. She was insistent on it, but I told her I didn't think it would work, but, you know, I wanted to make a good impression on everyone about the Seven Caves Touring Center and the town and… well, anyway, that took a couple of hours while we looked at carpet. I talked with Lester Rigby, and then went straight to Hitch-Morgan and talked with Lena Morgan, and then came here from there. Before that I was at Grovey Goodies with Trevor."

Deputy Dylan took this all in stride, making notes and nodding as he did. "And Trevor Simmons," he said after he'd finished writing, "did he go with you to Rigby's?"

Bailey blinked, and then shook her head. "No, he… he stayed behind. But, I don't think Trevor did this."

"We just have to cover all the bases," Dylan assured her, patient in the face of her plain anxiety. It was impressive, actually—there was a better than a good chance that this was the first murder investigation in Coven Grove in… well, maybe forever. Certainly not since Bailey was born. "Can you recall anyone who might have had a reason to attack Ms. Tells? Did you see any conflicts or arguments?"

Bailey sighed, and shook her head. "I'm afraid not.

Really—pardon me, I don't mean to speak ill of her—but I only knew her for a little while and she struck me as a little hard to deal with. She had a temper. So, I don't know if I could narrow down a list of people who might have disliked her. I'm sorry."

"It's okay," Dylan said. "Well, we may have more questions later. Take this," he handed her a card, "and call us if you remember anything else. I think Ave and your Daddy are over there; why don't you go see them, and try to take some time to process. It must have been real awful to find her like that."

Bailey only nodded. More than awful.

"Not this girl. Somebody else. Out of towner, probably one of the crew. Or the assistant, maybe."

"Who, Gloria?" Bailey asked.

"What's that?" Dylan asked, frowning. "Gloria's the assistant, right?"

"Yes," Bailey said, "I thought you just said…" Oh. It was back, those echoing whispers. Suddenly, she could hear them again, like the volume had been turned up so slowly she hadn't noticed. Now that she had, they were deafening. She rubbed her palms together and shook her head. "Never mind. I thought you asked me something."

"We'll get to the bottom of it, Ms. Robinson," Dylan assured her. "You just stand by and rest."

"I will, Deputy," Bailey told him. "Thank you."

He tipped his hat, and moved on.

Bailey tried to not-quite-run toward the line of police tape. When she was finally past it, she threw herself into her father's arms. Ryan squeezed her tight, and then held her at arms length and peered into her eyes like he might discern how she was feeling that way. "Lord, Red; you must be shook up. You okay?"

"Not really," Bailey said. Her throat was tight. She kept seeing Martha. And the voices she heard kept stirring her up all over again, but she couldn't tell him about that. Not yet; not until she knew more herself. He'd only worry himself to death.

Avery hugged her next, as tight as Ryan had, and whispered to her, "Who could have done this?"

Bailey let him release her and shook her head at him, a silent answer: No idea. His lips tightened, and he stared determinedly at the cave. Bailey glanced at the entrance as well. "They'll figure it out," she said to him. "It's a small town. People don't get away with that sort of thing in places like this."

One of the deputies was talking with Gloria. She looked pale, barely animated. Her curiosity too great, Bailey led Avery and her Father around the perimeter to get closer. They were just barely audible, but she caught bits and pieces.

"…up at the tour office," Gloria was saying, matter-of-factly, her voice flat. "Maybe… two, or three hours ago? She wanted me to get her dress pressed and steamed. Again. I went from there to the hotel."

"Was anyone with you?" The deputy asked.

Gloria fixed him with a flinty look of offense. "No, I was alone. But Martha was paying my salary, so, I'm jobless now, and my last boss was murdered, right? Why would I want to ruin my own career, again?"

The Deputy took it in stride. "I have to ask, Ma'am," he told her, scribbling on his official note pad, "it's the job. But, it would be best if you didn't leave town while the investigation is ongoing. Also, we don't know for sure she was murdered. Yet."

"Well, I'm not going anywhere in any case," Gloria said. "I'm going to help you get the bottom of this. I'm an investigative journalist, you know. Or, I was before I was Martha's assistant." Bailey knew it. Why the deception, though? And why go from journalist to assistant? For someone who was probably too broke to pay her nearly what she was used to, no less. Couldn't she have just come along as a reporter to cover the event for whatever paper she worked for?

Bailey's suspicions started to congeal.

Except, Trevor was on this side of the police line, a dozen yards away and speaking with another deputy. He kept rubbing his face, shaking his head, and fidgeting. Objectively, Bailey had to admit that he'd said some harsh things about Martha and clearly didn't like her very much. And, there was no telling where he'd gone after Bailey left him at the bakery. The bakery ladies would know, though; or at least they'd know when he left. She didn't see them in the small crowd. Probably they were too busy with the shop to come and ogle the scene.

The other conspicuous absence was Poppy. This sort of thing was going to shut down the tours for a good long while; she should have been out here throwing a fit about how Martha had been so rude as to die horribly at the start of prime tour season. Wasn't she at least worried about her bottom line? Maybe she hadn't heard yet.

Bailey tried to call her, but got no answer. Poppy's day-to-day life was a mystery; she came and went with the tide, sometimes. She'd want to know soon, though; this was going to cost her a lot of money, and if there was one thing Poppy absolutely hated, it was losing money.

She slipped her phone back into her pocket and watched Trevor with the Deputy. She wanted to get closer, but not look like she was doing it. Biting her lip, she glanced around, and then tugged at her father's hand. "Come on," she said. "I don't think they need us here anymore, and we'll just get in the way. I need to go lay down, I think."

"Of course, Red," Ryan said, and slipped his arm around her shoulder. He started to walk her toward the path back up to the office but she tugged him toward Trevor.

"Lets go around the crowd," she sighed. "I'd rather not

be accosted with questions. I don't know anything more than they do at this point."

Ryan agreed, and Avery followed them shortly as the three of them walked between two parked, white cars with the gold star of the Coven Grove Sheriff's department emblazoned on the sides. She took them to within a few yards of Trevor's interview. He met her eyes for just a brief second before he answered some question the deputy had asked. She strained to hear.

"I was at my hotel room," he said. "The whole time. No one was with me, though, so I understand. It's possible that the hotel clerk saw me walk in, but I can't know for sure. You'll have to ask her."

"I'll do that," the deputy said. "You sure there's no one else you talked to on the way? Even on the street. You say you walked? Which route did you take?"

"I just sort of wandered, honestly," Trevor answered, earnestly. "I don't recall exactly which route I took. I remember a house with a red door, though, and…"

They were out of range. Bailey wanted to stop, and go back, and listen in, but that would have been outrageously overt and Ryan would have seen right through it. She glanced up at him. Already there was a quiet light in his lined eyes, and he had his thinking face on. Avery did as well, both of them chewing things over, making their own theories.

On the walk back up, Bailey tried calling Poppy again. For the second time, she got no answer. A nervous feeling settled into her stomach. This was the sort of time when Poppy should have been hovering over every aspect of the office. Bailey hoped she was okay. She couldn't help thinking, suddenly, that something might have happened to the woman. After all, Martha was a washed up nobody, according to Trevor and Poppy both... but Poppy had money, and a business, and traveled all over. What if Martha had just been a casualty of something else? What if Poppy had been hurt or killed or abducted? After all, she had family with money.

The other possible explanation, of course, was that Poppy had killed Martha herself, but that was the furthest thing from likely that Bailey could imagine. Poppy was an awful person at times, and she certainly had a temper. But she was driven by something far more powerful than her emotions, or any urges she might harbor toward anyone; Bailey had seen her bend over backward in pursuit of her singular principle, sacrificing everything for it.

That principle, of course, was profit; and Martha's death would cost Poppy somewhere in the range of seventy-five thousand dollars. If anything, Poppy was probably holed up in some bar outside of town, weeping into a glass of cheap white wine and contemplating how ruined her business was going to be after this.

Only at that point did Bailey really think about it herself. She saw her dreams of taking over the tour business evaporate. Instantly, she felt guilty for it.

Martha Tells had died on their watch. That's what

mattered. That, and that somewhere in this town a murderer was running loose; someone that had desecrated her precious Caves and tainted them, in her mind, forever. And that person, she very much wanted to see brought to justice.

And, she determined at that moment, she'd do whatever she could to see that they were.

Chapter 7

The next two days were a blur to Bailey. As the person who'd found the body—no; found Martha, she couldn't think of Martha as 'the body' without her chest tightening—she was both the talk of the town, and the prime witness not just for the Sheriff's department, but for the local paper, the Coven Grove Weekly.

When Ryan had worked for them full time it had been the Coven Grove Daily, but that changed as the Internet reached the town and made a daily paper all but obsolete. Plus there was never much news to cover in Coven Grove—fairs, contests and who won them, local political news which was repetitive after several decades of seeing the same people hold offices until they passed or retired, just like Sheriff Larson.

Now that they had the scent of a real story, reporters were clamoring to pitch their various takes on it, including Gloria Olson. In the end, it was her that won first prize and got her story printed.

It wasn't news to Bailey that Martha Tells had been deeply in debt and hoping to reboot her career by coming home to exploit the caves, but it was news to everyone else. Overnight, it became the talk of the town—even more so than it already had been. Martha was the first murder victim in Coven Grove for as long as anyone could remember. She wasn't the first, however. Another article detailed the other six cases in the town's history, the last one more than eighty years ago. The strange thing, the article suggested, was that the one before it had happened only a year prior. In fact, all six of the murders of the early twentieth century were 'suspiciously' close together. Was Coven Grove potentially looking at a string of similar murders in the modern day?

Both articles were printed in papers that ran for two consecutive days, prompting Ryan to wonder whether the paper was going to use this event to re-re-brand themselves to a daily paper again. Either way, the two stories hurled the town into a rabid frenzy for details and gossip and very soon it was all anyone was talking about.

Bailey sequestered herself in the library. The initial enthusiasm and righteous sense of purpose she'd had about somehow single-handedly solving Martha's murder bled away with surprising speed once she'd had a night of troubled sleep and disconcerting dreams. It was best, she decided, to keep to herself. Especially since being out about town seemed to make the voices in her head worse while being in the library gave her a desperately needed break from that maelstrom of insanity though she couldn't figure why that would be. She was not left alone for very long. On the second day, just after lunchtime, Avery and Piper showed up to check on her. Avery was dressed a little smarter than usual, it seemed like—probably he'd been fielding questions as one of Bailey's two 'known associates'. Piper, of course, was nearly pregnant enough to pop already, only six months in. She managed it well, though; Piper was a woman who made pregnancy somehow look easy in her ankle length, flowing, forest green jersey knit one-piece that on anyone else would have looked like the moo-moo it technically was. But a clever braided brown leather belt and a matching brown cotton bolero turned it into something almost queenly and high fashion.

They brought the lunch that Bailey had skipped.

"I love you both so, so much," she announced as she unwrapped the sandwich and went to work on it. She hadn't realized how hungry she was. This was from Elliot's the deli, she assumed, and was phenomenal although that could have been her stomach talking. She liked what it was saying anyway.

Avery helped Piper into one of the chairs around the wide library table. It was littered with books about languages, iconography, and what little academic interest had been leveled at the Caves.

"So," Avery said casually, "how are you doing?"

"I can't imagine," Piper said, "finding a body like that? It must have been so awful, how are you sleeping?"

Bailey chewed and swallowed while she looked from one of them to the other. There were whispers again— far in the back of her head, but noticeable, like a mosquito buzzing around her ear. "I'm okay," she said. "It was scary, but, you know... I'm dealing. Any news?"

Avery and Piper shared a brief look, one of clear mutual concern. Avery reached across the table and touched Bailey's arm. "You know it's okay to not be okay, right?"

"I'm really fine," Bailey assured him, as earnestly as she could manage. "It was terrible, of course, and scary but… I can't just dwell on it. I'm moving forward."

"By hiding in here?" Piper asked, grimacing as though she expected Bailey to snap at her in response.

Piper wasn't always like that. Things must have been getting worse at home. Bailey sighed, and put her sandwich down, and tucked hair behind her ears. "I'm concerned about what it's going to do to the town. And about Martha, and her getting justice. You saw the article, right? Eighty years since there was a murder in Coven Grove. I know that Sheriff Larson has a lot of experience, and I know he even has a masters in criminal justice—"

"Er, it's a bachelor's," Avery corrected; he didn't seem confident it would be enough.

"Well, whatever—he's been the Sheriff for a long time but… well he's a local, born and raised here. I'm worried he just doesn't know what to do about this. And every day he doesn't figure this out is a day that either there's a murderer out there on the run, getting away with what they did; or there's a murderer in our town. And who knows who'll be next? What if it's a serial killer and this was just the beginning?"

The two of them stared at Bailey, eyebrows having slowly risen as she let it all out.

Bailey sighed. "I've had a lot of time to think about it."

"We can see that," Piper said. She frowned. "You're not okay, are you?"

Bailey waved her off and took another bite of her sandwich to avoid another rant.

"Well I haven't been okay," Avery said seriously. "So I've been thinking about all the evidence assembled so far." It was very little. "I think we need to take a clear, critical look at everyone who associated with Martha since she arrived in town and figure out who doesn't fit—or who might have had an agenda."

"We've been compiling a list," Piper said. She pulled something from the top of her dress, stowed presumably in the bra that covered her ample bosom. She was known to produce all manner of oddities from there; Bailey never quite got that developed, and was as mystified by this ongoing magic trick as Avery often was.

Bailey stared at the folded slip of paper. "Have you taken it to Sheriff Larson?"

"Of course we did," Avery said. "We took it to him first thing. He said to leave it to the department."

"Well, maybe we should," Bailey said around a mouthful of sandwich. "It's their jurisdiction. We don't have jurisdiction."

"There's such a thing as citizen's arrest," Piper supplied. "I read about it. Oregon state law has provisions for civilian investigation and even arrests with appropriate evidence, of course. It's been on the books for ages, from back when this was all frontier."

They were really serious about this. Bailey put her sandwich back down again, and took the list. She unfolded it. "This is... a long list."

"Well, we figured you could help us narrow it down," Avery said, excited to be investigating a murder.

"From everyone in town?" Bailey wondered. It was a very long list.

Piper shrugged. "We got carried away, maybe."

Bailey opened one of the books she'd collected and took back the pen she'd used as a temporary book mark, and started picking down the list and circling names she thought were worth considering.

Avery tugged the book toward him and looked it over. "Wow. Thinking about making another go at translating the writing in the Caves? That takes me back..."

"Let me see," Piper said. She looked through the section Bailey had bookmarked, lips pursed with interest.

Bailey finished her assessment of the list. Circled on it now were Trevor, Gloria, Poppy, 'crewmen'—Piper and Avery didn't know any of the ACT crewman's names, of course—and at the bottom, written in, Bailey herself.

Avery's eyebrows creased. "Are you a suspect?"

"I found the body," she said. "The person who finds the body is always a suspect. How do you know I didn't kill Martha myself and call it in to keep from being suspected."

"Why would anyone kill someone and then call the police?" Piper asked, incredulous. "It doesn't make sense."

"Exactly. And neither of you thought to put my name on the list because you're biased in my favor—not because you were thinking it through rationally."

Avery and Piper shared a look, and then stared at Bailey.

"Did you kill Martha?" Avery asked carefully.

Bailey rolled her eyes. "Of course not—that's not the point. The point is, we know everyone in town. Everyone knows everyone here, it makes it hard to be objective. It's not as easy as just pointing people out and following 'clues'. This isn't a Poirot story, and we're not the police."

"We can still help," Piper said sullenly. She winced suddenly and put her hand to her round belly. "James agrees, I think. That, or he's cranky, one or the other."

She breathed through it.

"She's right," Avery said. "And maybe baby James, too. We should be doing something. The whole town should be banding together over this."

"Over what?" A pleasant voice called from the doorway, slightly ajar as Chloe poked her head through. She entered the rest of the way, carrying a small box that no doubt had something delicious inside. "Hi, kids," she said, smiling broadly, "what are you all talking about?" She glanced at the books on the table, and frowned. "The Caves?"

"We were just gossiping, Chloe," I said. "Piper and Avery think—"

Avery shot me a warning look.

"—that I should focus on something… distracting and academic to try and get over finding Martha," I finished.

The whispers got a little louder, but not more numerous. They were suspicious, I thought, nattering on about… about Chloe? Don't trust her, they seemed to say, don't trust anyone, everyone's a suspect, she came in at a convenient time, didn't she? Bailey had to squeeze her eyes closed and rub her temples.

"Everything okay?" Chloe asked.

"Just a headache," Bailey muttered. She shook two more aspirin from a bottle that was almost gone—she'd picked it up the same day she'd found Martha—and swallowed them down without water. Funny how easy that got with practice.

Chloe nodded slowly. "Sorry I haven't been by," she said. "But I was thinking about you. I brought you a cupcake. Actually, a couple. I made one yesterday but... didn't see you so, I figured I'd bring them to you."

In fact, Chloe had never visited Bailey here before—or anywhere else, for that matter. It seemed more than a little odd, but Bailey was mostly just thankful for a distraction from Avery and Piper's crusade.

"How did you know she'd be at the library?" Avery asked, feigning casual disinterest in the answer.

"Because Bailey retreats to the library when she'd stressed," Chloe said slowly, confused at the question. "Everyone knows that."

Piper shrugged, and nodded and then peeked in the box Chloe sat down on the table between the three of them.

"Thanks, Chloe," Bailey said. A cupcake didn't quite seem to appeal at the moment, but maybe it would later.

"So," Chloe said. "How are you getting along?"

"That's the question of the day," Bailey groaned. "I'm okay, really—that's for all of you. Bailey Robinson will be fine."

"Good," Chloe said. "That's good. What all did you see in there? If you don't mind my asking."

"It was all in the paper," Bailey sighed.

"I saw. But, nothing you left out?"

The three of them tried to act as casual as they could. Avery and Piper busied themselves with the cupcakes. The ones that were for Bailey were obvious—they were the most decorated

"I don't think so," Bailey answered. Or, she thought she did. It was getting hard to hear anything over those whispers.

"Any odd smells?" Chloe asked. "Sulfur, or… herbs, anything like that?"

Bailey caught the sharp eye Avery gave her and shook her head. "No. Nothing like that."

Chloe nodded slowly, seemingly thinking about something. Her eyes settled on Avery, and she sighed. It seemed strange—not like Chloe at all to seem so… irritated? Maybe nervous?

"Well, I'm glad you're doing okay," she said to Bailey. "Ave, Piper; I'll see you two around. The three of you come by the bakery later on—get this girl out of the library and into the sun sometime, it'll do her good." She winked at Bailey and they all exchanged pleasant, if tight, goodbyes.

When Chloe was gone, Avery leaned in and whispered loud enough that anyone outside the door probably could have heard him anyway. "Oh my God Chloe Minds totally killed Martha!"

"What?" Bailey said. "No, don't be… that's ridiculous. Why on earth would Chloe have killed Martha?"

"Well I don't know, Bee, but you can't tell me that wasn't suspicious as heck!" He glanced over his shoulder like she might come back any minute. "She wanted to know what you smelled? Why would she ask for a detail like that unless she had some idea of what happened? Maybe she was trying to see if you remembered some key piece of evidence or something; the thing that would implicate her. We should totally follow her, see if she's up to anything suspicious."

"He does have a point," Piper mused. Suspecting Chloe of murder hadn't kept her from enjoying a peanut-butter cupcake, though. She licked frosting off her lower lip.

"You two… it just can't possibly be Chloe."

"Are you sure you aren't just biased?" Avery asked. He tapped the list. "You had a good point. We have to be objective about this."

Bailey struggled to ignore the whispers. They were receding again, but slowly. Honestly, she wasn't sure she could even be rational right now. But she took Avery's point and tried to set aside any feelings she had about anyone. It took some convincing, but ultimately she was able to admit to herself that the whole visit had been unusual.

"Alright," she said finally. "If I'm being entirely objective… then, yes. It was odd. Good grief, I don't know if I could deal with that…" But she penned Chloe's name at the bottom of the list, right under her own, and circled it. "The bakery isn't far. Maybe she walked. If we go quickly, we should be able to keep an eye on her."

The three of them scampered out of the chairs—well, Avery helped Piper up, anyway, but he scampered for the both of them—and the trio peeked out the door before they went out into town, hot on the trail of their first real suspect in the murder of Martha Tells.

Bailey sighed to herself as they attempted the pursuit. This is all going end very badly, she thought through the growing storm of voices in her head. I just know it.

Chapter 8

They did manage to keep an eye on Chloe. She had
walked to the Library, of course—there was no reason
to drive such a short distance—but rather than rub her
hands with obviously sinister glee or duck into any non-
existent dark alleys or some secret lair like Bailey
thought her friends possibly expected, she merely
walked back to Grovey Goodies and, presumably, went
back to work. She did have a job, after all.

Avery wasn't convinced. He rubbed his bare chin as
though there should have been a goatee there for him to
scratch ponderously. "What if all three of them were in
on it?" He wondered out loud.

"That's a leap," Piper sighed. Between their first
uneventful tailing, the midday heat, and her unborn
child, her energy had pretty much waned at this point.
Still, she was trying to maintain some enthusiasm. "I
could bring the minivan, and we could stake her out."

Bailey groaned, and shook her head. "She knows what
your minivan looks like, Piper."

"Well we could borrow her mother-in-law's car,"
Avery suggested brightly. You'd think he was planning
a surprise party instead of a stake out of a beloved
neighbor. "She never drives it, right?"

"I am absolutely not asking Gavin's mother for her

car, Ave." That line of inquiry was neatly nipped in the bud. Avery put his hands up in surrender in the face of Piper's instantly darkened mood. He made a mental note...don't poke a pregnant gal when she's hot, tired and cranky.

"Maybe we should just call it quits for now," Bailey said. "Chloe's going to be there until they close like she always is. What's the point of hanging around outside the bakery when she can't leave."

"Why couldn't she leave?" Avery asked. "She came to the library."

"And I'll admit that was suspicious," Bailey agreed. "But she's not going to be running around town making herself look more like a suspect, now is she?"

He shrugged, tilted his head to think about it and then sighed, slumping a little. "You're probably right. So what next, then?"

Bailey looked from Piper to Avery and back. They were both looking at her for an answer. "How am I supposed to know? We keep our eyes peeled, I guess."

"They make this look a lot more interesting on Law and Order," Piper commented.

"And CSI," Avery added. "We need forensic evidence or something to throw science at until we get an answer."

Bailey was sure he was mostly joking, but she couldn't bring herself to laugh. That whispering was getting worse and worse the longer she was out of the library. She very much wanted to go back.

But, the truth of the matter was that Chloe had been acting suspiciously. As much as it pained her to imagine that the woman might have done something so awful… how much did she really know about Chloe Minds? Almost nothing. The same went for Aria and Frances. Those three women were well known in the community in general—they donated to bakes sales, had shown up for city council meetings, and were known to have an open door policy all around for anyone who needed an ear to pull.

But in all that, Bailey couldn't honestly say she knew who any of them really were. They didn't seem to have family in town, none of them were married, and come to think of it, Bailey wasn't even sure where they lived.

As involved as the women of the Grovey Goodies bakery were with Coven Grove… they might as well have been strangers. There was something so odd about that. Who knew what other secrets they might be hiding?

"You two should go home," Bailey said finally. "Piper, you need to get off your feet. And Avery… you're probably better off researching Martha's past, anyway. Plus I think you're going to burn up in this sun. Would hate to see that snow white skin of yours get a little color." She winked at him.

Avery feigned scandal, and checked his pale arms for signs of any such thing. He shrugged, and squinted at the afternoon light. "Well… you make a strong argument for being back indoors," he said. "I'll see what I can find on Martha. Maybe talk to that Gloria woman she came here with."

"Just be careful," Piper said. "Gloria's a suspect, don't forget."

"Well she can't just go on a murder spree and nobody notice," Avery argued. "Plus, you both know I have a special way with the ladies." He waggled his eyebrows suggestively, and Piper and Bailey both giggled at him.

"Sure you wouldn't be better off interviewing Trevor?" Bailey suggested.

Avery pressed his hand to his chest, wounded. "That man is too handsome to kill anybody. I won't believe it. Still… good point. I might talk to both of them...they probably picked up different things."

"Well, Bailey's right about me getting off my feet," Piper said. "You two call me if you find anything out. My feet are killing me. I might drop back by the library though. Gavin's mother is a mean old hag to me, but she never gets tired of Riley at least. I intend to enjoy my break." She glanced at her belly. "Such as it is, anyway."

Bailey made an effort not to glance at Avery. The bitterness in Piper's voice wasn't new, but it was getting worse and worse over time. She didn't like them to pry, though, so they didn't. For now.

"I'll see you both later then," Bailey said. They traded

hugs and kisses on cheeks and Avery walked with Piper back toward the library, their first amateur sleuthing attempt sorely unsuccessful.

"…locked my keys in my car…"

"…could be cheatin' on me with that floozy Candice…"

"…if Thomas would even notice if I…"

"…so pretty I could just…"

Bailey pressed her hands to her head and tried to focus on her breathing. It was all so loud. Why was it happening? She wished her Dad were with her. Suddenly she wanted to tell him everything that was on her mind, all of her worries. He claimed not to know anything about her mother, but maybe he at least knew how they could check hospital records, maybe find some instance of a crazy lady having a psychotic break.

That would make sense, wouldn't it? That her mother had gone off the deep end, and Bailey had been given up because she wasn't fit to take care of an infant? Coven Grove didn't have a psychiatric facility like an asylum, but there was one further inland—Lakeview Heights, maybe an hour and a half east. What if all this time her mother had been there? Crazy ran in families, after all, sometimes.

The worst of it, though, was a much darker kind of fear. A secret, nagging worry in the back of her mind that had been festering since just a few hours after she found Martha, when the crowds had gathered.

What if… what if she'd been right to put herself on the suspect list? What if she really was losing her mind, and had blacked out and…

She shook her head, and squeezed her eyes tight against the sudden welling of tears that burned her eyes. It couldn't be. She couldn't have done something like that, surely, no matter what was going on inside her brain.

Bailey realized she was standing on the sidewalk, still, about to start bawling her eyes out. She rubbed them, and looked around her. She wanted to be alone.

Despite the terrible thing that had happened there, she found herself walking back toward the Caves. Underneath the dread she felt at going back there, though, was that same familiar tug; the promise of solitude, and calm, and a little bit of peace. Plus, the last time she'd started hearing the voices and gone there, they'd quieted a little bit.

Just now, she needed that, desperately.

It was a long walk, but it helped to calm Bailey down so she didn't mind. She checked the Tour office when she got there, but it was still locked, no sign of Poppy. That was worrying, but with everything else going on, and Bailey's world started to feel like it was coming apart at the seams—inside and out—and she couldn't muster up the will to ruminate on it.

The police tape was gone from the entrance of the

caves. Martha had been removed, of course, and taken to the coroner's office. They'd had to call in an out-of-towner. Coven Grove no longer had a resident coroner because death around here was categorically natural in some way, and very rarely unexpected.

She wandered cautiously into the entrance to the caves, but dared not walk much further than the first one. The voices had grown distant the closer she got to them, and when she was deep into the first wide cavern they finally quieted all together. Blessed relief.

Bailey lowered herself to the cool cave floor, and leaned back against one of the unadorned walls not roped off with the fancy red velvet ropes that only looked like actual velvet—they were cheap, like everything else Poppy bothered to put any money into. She leaned her head back against the stone, and listened to the distant crash of waves funneling up through the caves at high tide.

She might have drifted off. She wasn't entirely sure, but when she opened her eyes seemingly a moment later, the light at the entrance of the Caves was much dimmer, almost dark. She must have dozed off, then, it looked like it might be getting on into the evening.

Though she didn't really feel like she'd napped at all, Bailey stood and brushed the back of her jeans off and decided she should probably head home. Ryan would be worried about her, especially now. She was a little surprised he hadn't already come looking for her.

When she got outside the Caves and looked up at the

sky, she realized that it wasn't merely getting late in the evening—the clear blue sky from the afternoon had clouded over with a surprise bank of thick, roiling clouds that looked darkly gray with the promise of a surprise deluge. The weather on the coast was finicky like that but… she'd recalled that the next week was due to be pretty clear. And come to think of it, she hadn't noticed the clouds rolling in from the ocean. Normally you could see them miles off, unobstructed by the flat, featureless Pacific.

The wind picked up quickly as Bailey began the trek back up to town, and when it bit at her face she turned a little to keep it from her eyes, her hand held up as her hair whipped around her head.

That's when she saw someone, out next to the great oak that had managed, somehow, to stay firmly attached to the earth above the steep, short cliffs down to the beach, an ancient sentinel to watch over the Seven Caves that wound through the rocky coastlines' interior. She squinted. Was that Frances? What was Frances doing out here in this weather?

She was doing something… odd. She had her arms up, and then she swayed them in the air one way, and then the other, and then dropped them. Then, like a conductor calling the orchestra to raise their instruments and play, she lifted her hands again. At that precise moment, coincidentally, the wind gusted again, and howled through the cliffs and whistled though the Seven Caves like a ghostly chorus.

That sound… Bailey knew it well. You could hear it

throughout Coven Grove when it stormed, and she'd often opened her window at home and leaned out to listen to it. Then, as now, it sounded like a call to her, personally. That was silly, she knew, as she had since she'd begun the process of growing up and letting go of her childish notions. But now, more than ever, she felt it call to her, deep down in some place she almost felt like she recognized. A place she had forgotten about when she grew up.

As she watched, Frances threw something over the cliffs, and Bailey's heart leapt. The murder weapon, perhaps? It was the first thought that sprang to mind, but instantly vanished as she saw that it seemed to be handfuls of something light enough to rise up on the wind and fly off into the sky over the ocean.

Frances left the tree, and walked along the cliffs toward the Caves; but not to the front entrance. Bailey crouched, and scuttled off the path to watch from behind a thin bush—it didn't seem like much in the way of a hiding spot, but Frances wasn't looking her direction anyway—and then Bailey saw that Frances wasn't alone.

Chloe and Aria were with her.

Bailey's stomach turned, and her heart twisted. Avery had been right. The three of them… they all had something to do with Martha's murder. But what were they doing here now? Cleaning up the evidence, Bailey supposed.

The three women turned together, clutching their coats

against the wind, and headed down the cliffs. As soon as they were out of sight, driven by some sudden burst of courage and anger, Bailey dashed out from behind her bush and down the path. She pressed against the outer rock of the Caves' entrance, and peeked around the corner. When the coast seemed clear, she padded along the rocky outcrop, picking her way carefully to avoid dislodging any stones and making a clatter. Soon she was positioned over the three women who were holding hands in front of…

Bailey blinked. It was like an optical illusion. She'd seen this patch of rock before. She knew the whole area by heart. Except… she could swear that was another cave entrance. It wouldn't quite stay still for her, somehow—it slipped one way and the other, or her eyes did, and instead she had to focus on the three women; in this way, she could sort of see the gap in the rock face in her peripheral vision.

What were they doing?

Almost the moment she wondered, Chloe raised her head, eyebrows creased with concern until they slackened when she looked straight at Bailey, shock and dismay on her face. The two other women looked up at her next, and their mouths opened, but the wind was too loud to make out what they were saying.

And Bailey didn't stick around to find out. She turned on the rocks, stumbled a little as she scrambled back up, toward the path to town, and then took off at a dead run.

Chapter 9

"Bailey!" Someone called after her as she ran. "Bailey, wait! You don't understand!"

Bailey heaved breaths into her lungs, fighting the wind for every foot of distance she gained up the path. It seemed almost like a living thing, intent on hindering her progress. The voice calling for her from behind— Chloe, she thought—seemed to get closer and closer though, unencumbered by the gale.

When a hand grabbed her shoulder and tugged her to a stop, Bailey turned around, swinging. Chloe was every bit as wind-swept as Bailey was, and she cringed back when Bailey swung an arm at her.

"It was you!" Bailey howled. "You killed Martha! How could you?"

Bailey may as well have landed a blow; Chloe looked like she'd been kicked in the stomach. The wind died down, vanishing as though it had never been. "Bailey... of course I didn't kill Martha. How could you think that about me? You know me."

Stay objective, Bailey tried to remind herself. Of course a murderer wouldn't admit to being a murderer. At the same time... suddenly, all the pieces that had fit so neatly together seemed more jagged and mismatched than she'd thought just moments before. It wasn't as though the women were going into the cave where Martha was actually killed... but that did raise other questions all the same, and Bailey's suspicions simply found a new foothold.

"What were you all doing back there, then?" She asked. Chloe took a step toward her, reaching out with one hand, but Bailey paced her, keeping distance between them.

Chloe paused, and then lowered her hand, and ultimately clasped both of them together over her stomach. "We were looking for evidence of what happened to Martha," she said. "A long time ago we… well we were all friends. We want to find out what happened to her, but we don't think the Sheriff's department is likely to be much help."

Funny, really. The three ladies on their little quest, and Bailey with her two friends. Two trios skulking around, trying to unearth the truth. Except, it seemed the bakery ladies had more practice.

Bailey saw Aria and Frances come around the caves and pause at the bottom of the path. She looked carefully at Chloe. "Frances… before, at the tree she looked like she was…" The thought of saying it out loud almost made Bailey laugh. It was a ridiculous thought. That Frances had somehow summoned up a storm? "Never mind," she said instead, waving it off. She ran her fingers through her hair, tugging handfuls of it to relieve that awful headache that was near to splitting her head in two.

"It looks like she was controlling the weather," Chloe said. She spoke tentatively, with hesitation and care, as though the words themselves might somehow do Bailey harm if they were spoken too quickly. She glanced back down the path at her friends. Then she took a step toward Bailey, closing a little distance.

Bailey let her, confused, and in pain, and overcome with a sudden dizziness that made her regret having eaten before. "I don't feel well," she muttered.

Chloe took her shoulders and held her steady. She ducked her head to meet Bailey's eyes, and squinted at her. There was an odd feeling in Bailey's head, like an itch she wouldn't have been able to scratch had she been inclined to try. Some of the headache, however, receded.

"Oh, dear," Chloe said; softly, though, and compassionately. She sighed. "You've been hearing voices."

Bailey's eyes snapped up. "Why would you think that? Oh, Lord… I'm crazy, aren't I? You can tell just by looking at me. I knew it…"

Chloe's laugh was sympathetic if amused, and she shook her head slowly. "Oh, my dear… no. You're not crazy, Bailey. You're… gifted. Come back with me. Talk with the three of us. You probably have so many questions and we can answer them, sweetheart." She raised a hand when Bailey began to argue. "We can stay in the open. We really don't mean you any harm."

There was something. Some sense of belonging or connection that Bailey couldn't quite put her finger on, and couldn't quite discount either. She looked to where Aria and Frances waited. These women; she'd know them since she was small. They had always been kind to her, always patient. Their presence, and especially Chloe's had been so important to her after Wendy passed. Didn't she at least owe them a chance to explain, after all that?

"Alright," Bailey finally sighed.

Chloe smiled, and put an arm around her shoulder as she guided Bailey back down to the other women.

Once there, however, Frances fixed Chloe with a flinty look, and jerked her chin a bit. "A word?"

"I won't be long," Chloe said.

Aria went with them. Though they were only a few feet away, Bailey couldn't hear what they were saying. The sound just didn't carry. It seemed the strangest thing—like they were on mute. She found herself sticking a finger in either ear, but then, she could hear the ocean just fine. They spoke for a few minutes, and when they were done Aria and Frances gave Bailey polite smiles and good-byes, and went their own way.

Bailey was left alone with Chloe. For a long moment, they stood there, near one another but quiet.

Just as Bailey was about to break the silence with a question, Chloe spoke.

"You know, this town is very old. Older, in fact, than the country itself is. Before it was Coven Grove, it was a little settlement with no name. Before that it was a kind of village. Before even that, it was just a meeting place, but there was always someone here." She glanced at the nearby caves, and waved a finger at them. "Those Caves… they've been calling people to this place for a long, long time."

She watched Bailey's face for a moment, and then looked out over the sea. "You've always been drawn to them," she said. It was no secret, of course—everyone in town knew how much Bailey loved the caves, especially after she took over the tours. But Chloe knew more than just that. "When you were just a girl, you thought they were magic. You hoped, anyway. And sometimes, when you were in them, you thought you heard whispers coming from the paintings; like they were alive. Am I right?"

Stunned, Bailey could only nod slowly. She'd never told anyone that. How did Chloe know?

"Not everyone can hear those whispers. I haven't even heard them in… oh, more than twenty years now. You won't hear them forever, you see. Just when you're very young. No one's quite sure why. There was a time, though, when someone would have noticed, and they would have known that it was time." She sighed, sad. "I suppose, given that your mother wasn't around for you, there was no one to notice."

Bailey's heart sped up a bit. She straightened, and suddenly the urgency that filled her pushed away all other concerns. "Chloe… did you know my mother? My birth mother, I mean?"

Chloe smiled, a distant, fond memory, but maybe one

laced with old hurt, too. "I wish I could say I did," she said. "It was a long time ago, though."

Just as quickly as she'd gotten excited, she felt her hopes fall and crumble. "Well, what do you mean about the whispers, and being noticed? Lately... well I'm hearing whispers again. Only louder and not in the Caves. If anything, being in there gives me a little peace. Up in town, though, and wherever there are people, it gets so loud. My head has been killing me for days now. I'm losing my mind, Chloe."

"Not exactly," Chloe said. She smiled slightly, not a happy smile exactly, but not entirely sad either. Conciliatory. "You're just finding other minds, and you don't quite know where to put them yet."

Bailey stared, and then looked at the ground, and finally turned her gaze out over the sea. Well... she'd somehow thought Chloe might be able to help. It turned out she was crazy, too. Maybe it was in the water...

Chloe chuckled, and put her hand on Bailey's shoulder. "You're not far off," she said. "But it's not in the water. It's in the caves. From way back. Old, old magic. Primal, from when the earth was new, and it sort of collects in a few places. These caves are one of those places. I'm not crazy, Bailey and neither are you. The magic here, in these caves—the magic you always believed in as a girl—you were touched with it when you were born. A single seed that took root and grew with you and is finally blossoming."

Twenty two. Bailey chanted the number in her mind

over and over again.

Chloe sighed. "Alright. Twenty two."

Fourteen.

"Fourteen."

One thousand two hundred and seventy…

"One thousand, two hundred and seventy…"

Six.

"…Six. Is that enough?"

Bailey staggered away. "You… but then you… how…"

Chloe sighed heavily, and wandered toward the outcropping that was the outer shell of the first cave. She turned when she came close to it, and leaned back against it, her arms folded over her chest. "The gift you have, the gift of Reading, and probably Glimpsing, later on, is the same as mine. Or very similar. It's a little different for each of us. And for all anyone knows it's just the beginning; the first of many such gifts. There's no way to predict it. Especially with you."

"Why especially me? And who is 'anyone'?"

The first question, Chloe only saved away with dismissive fingers, but the second she answered with a quiet smile. "Anyone who's a witch."

Bailey glanced up the path, toward town, where

Frances and Aria had gone. "So you... and Frances... and Aria, you're all... you're witches?"

"And you, it seems," Chloe said. "Yes."

"Are there others?" Bailey asked.

"A few," Chloe admitted. "You'll meet them, eventually. And there are others, elsewhere in the world, far and wide. Not a great many; there never have been. This world is full of wonders you only ever dreamed of, my love."

For a moment, Bailey was small again. "Here's a special treat just for you, my love." It had been what Chloe always said to her when Wendy first took her to Grovey Goodies, just days after it had opened.

What was she so afraid of? This was Chloe. It was Frances, and Aria. Witches or no—she wasn't sold on that—she knew these women. They were her friends.

"What did you think you could find here?" Bailey asked her. "You said you knew Martha from before. Before what? Do you know something about why she died?"

Chloe stood up from the rock, and shook her head. "That's what we hoped to find out tonight. The chances of finding anything were extremely small to begin with. The Caves don't often like to talk, even under dire circumstances."

"They talk?" Bailey asked, skeptical of the claim.

"As I said," Chloe replied, "not often. They're stubborn, most of the time. That's the way of very old things. As to Martha… she was one of us. Years ago, before she left."

Chloe shook her head sadly. "She used her gifts to gain some degree of fame. When it grew, she believed she might fare better out there. In the wider world.

"We told her it wouldn't work," Chloe said. "Our magic, our craft, is tied to the Caves. Here, we're strong. Out there, it wanes. Martha didn't believe it. Worse, she became… petulant. She came here to expose the truth about the caves, and about us."

Bailey frowned. Keeping a secret seemed to her like a rather classic, even cliche, motive for murder to her. "Alright," Bailey said, hesitantly and aware that she was walking on slippery ground. "So, Martha came back to expose… you all, as witches? And then she died…"

"We had nothing to do with that," Chloe said again, more firmly. "We couldn't have. The magic of the caves it… well, suffice it to say that none of us could have killed Martha. Not even because we wouldn't have done such a thing—which we wouldn't have, none of us—but because we could not physically accomplish such a thing inside the Caves. You have to believe me, Bailey." She seemed calm, almost more instructive than desperate.

Perhaps that was because of her next suggestion. Chloe closed the distance between them again, and pursed her lips. "I can prove it to you," she said. "If you want, you're welcome to read my mind. I can show you how. It won't be so easy with everyone, but our gift is similar. It will come more easily with me, with guidance."

What if it was true, Bailey wondered. What if she really had been right all along. What if there was magic, and she had it? What if Chloe was just what she claimed to be? Some part of it was terrifying, of course; it raised all kinds of questions. If magic and witches were real, then what else was real? Not all fairy tales were happy, after all.

Bailey had grown from an imaginative little girl, full of wonder and faith in the unseen part of the world, to a young woman who preferred cold, hard facts and evidence. Accepting the idea of magic seemed somehow immature. Like she was being gullible. But at the same time, if Chloe claimed to be able to offer her proof…

"Alright," Bailey said. "What do I do?"

Chloe smiled again. The clouds were beginning to clear. A shaft of sunlight fell on them, and Bailey had the thought that it seemed almost unreasonably portentous. Chloe didn't seem to notice. "Just close your eyes," she said, "and listen to my voice. I'll guide you to your gift. I'm going to touch your temples just so." She did, a light, airy touch as Bailey's eyes fluttered closed.

"Focus on my fingers," Chloe said softly, her voice easing into a neutral, rhythmic tone. "Count backward from ten. Each count brings you closer and closer to my voice, and to the sensation on your temples. Take long, deep breaths. Let yourself feel as though your feet are rooted in the Earth below you… sinking deep… drawing all those loud, noisy minds down, and down, into the ground…"

Chloe's voice had a strange quality to it. It echoed inside Bailey's head, lingering like the tingling leftovers of a light touch to the skin. "Now follow the touch of my fingers, and feel me here, in front of you. Feel the warmth coming from my presence… listen to where my voice is coming from… have you ever known you are not alone in a room? That nervous, subtle feeling of having someone nearby… focus on that feeling… open your eyes, Bailey."

Bailey did.

"Can you hear me?"

It was Chloe's voice, and she had undoubtedly spoken the words—she even raised her eyebrows as if the body language was all there like normal, except… her lips hadn't moved.

"Ask me," Chloe said, again without moving her lips. It wasn't some clever trick, either; her lips were sealed, pressed tightly together and in a tight grin of excitement when she saw Bailey's eyes widen.

Bailey knew instinctively what she meant; what she wanted Bailey to ask. "Did you, or Aria or Frances, have anything to do with Martha's death?"

"No, Bailey," Chloe said in her mind, which is what it had to be, "we didn't kill Martha Tells. She was our elder sister, and precious to us even if she did lose her way."

When she heard the words out loud, they were merely words. Spoken directly, however, mind to mind as it were, Bailey knew them to be true. They were not just words. They were impressions, concentrations of information that had texture and weight to them as they trickled into her mind.

Chloe hadn't killed Martha. It was a relief. But, then, who had?

"That's the question," Chloe's voice said in Bailey's mind. It was heavy and deep blue with the need to know the answer.

Bailey gazed into Chloe's eyes, captivated by the moment, by this surreal exchange, and it seemed as though, for half a second, she might fall into them. She saw a glittering cave, and an old woman knitting something, and a baby and—

Chloe let her temples go, and all of it faded like a dream, and just as impossible to hold onto. The images became muddy, and distant, and mist, and then were gone.

"What was that?" Bailey asked.

Chloe rubbed her forehead. She was sweating. "An indication that we already have quite a rapport. It's not uncommon. You probably just got a little backwash. If you think about how busy your mind normally is, it makes sense. At any given time, people are focusing on one particular thought—that inner monologue we all run around with—but that's just where our attention is. The reality of reading minds can be rather frustrating. You have to learn to sift through the extraneous chatter and focus on just what you want to hear. Not just what person, but what particular thought in each person."

She smiled, looking suddenly a bit tired. "You'll learn. And quickly, I imagine."

Bailey's body felt light. Whatever chore the connection had been for Chloe, it had imbued every inch of Bailey with sudden excitement. "Well this is perfect," she said, feeling her earlier sense of purpose congeal into a white hot fire of immanent justice. "All we have to do is interview people in town one at a time and listen for some admission, some indication that they killed Martha. It must be the only thing whoever did it can think about, right? If they're still in town. I know when I do something wrong—not that I do, of course; at least nothing really wrong—I feel just awful about it until I fess up. Surely the killer must—"

Chloe was laughing, the lines of her eyes showing as it reached them. "Don't you think I might have thought about that, little one?" She shook her head. "For one, it isn't as easy as you would think, and I've been doing it a lot longer than you. People's need to guard a secret can mask their thoughts from us. If someone is guilty enough, and actually wants to be caught, then it's possible but that's not very likely."

Bailey's excitement did flounder a little bit. What was the point of reading minds if you couldn't read minds when people didn't want you to? It suddenly seemed a great deal less useful.

"More importantly," Chloe went on, "reading thoughts isn't something that's exactly admissible in court. We need more than stray thoughts, and it's very difficult to tell the difference between memory and imagination in any case. And if we allow the true killer to catch on that we might be able to pry out his or her secret, well… I'm afraid that would put us on a pretty short list of follow up victims, don't you?"

Bailey hadn't thought of that. Well… five minutes as a witch and already it was a great deal more complicated than she'd imagined such things would be when she was a little girl. Things are always simpler when you're little.

"So," she asked Chloe, her face screwed up with new frustration, "then what do we do next?"

"Magic is a tool," Chloe said, "not a solution. We do what anyone who wants to solve a murder does. We investigate the old fashioned way."

Now that was disappointing. Still, as they walked up the path toward town in the failing evening light—now that the clouds had dispersed, it seemed that Bailey had in fact napped in the cave—it was hard to feel entirely let down, even if there was still a deep, nagging uncertainty about Chloe that Bailey just couldn't seem to let go of. At least, not just yet.

Chapter 10

The walk back to town, and then through a fading evening that settled into night by the time they reached the bakery, was done in relative silence. Bailey had questions—hundreds of them, it seemed—but the closer they came to the heart of Coven Grove, the more insistent and distracting the cacophony of other people's thoughts became.

"You've got to focus on your own thoughts," Chloe urged her when Bailey informed her of the noise in her head. "Try to hear them to the exclusion of all else. You're observant; that's why you keep tuning into everyone. It's in your nature to pay attention to everything, so you need to learn to pay attention only to what you want."

Bailey nodded, but that was no easy task. That Martha's murder meant there was a killer on the loose was bad enough; now that she was considering the many reasons why keeping a secret like this was critically necessary, her paranoia had begun to grow and she found herself watching the world around them, looking for people who were watching a little too closely or paying them too much interest.

More than that, though, she was desperately worried about having to keep this secret from her father, and her best friends. "They would never tell anyone about me," Bailey had said to Chloe, when the older witch categorically forbid her to tell them about herself. "They're my friends. I don't want to push them away."

"You won't have to," Chloe assured her.

But Bailey didn't believe it. "I can't name one person I've seen you in the company of other than Aria and Frances," she said. "I love the three of you—I do, Chloe—but I need Avery and Piper in my life. They helped me through the most painful times of my life. They've given me so much, and been my support system; I can't keep a secret from them like this."

Chloe had sighed, and told her to at least give it some time before she made a decision. She might understand later, when she knew more about their collective past— the history of the witches.

Bailey was really only concerned about one particular element of that history. "This... gift, if that's what it is; did I get it from my mother?"

Chloe was quiet for a moment, and then nodded once. "That's usually how it works. There are exceptions. Not everyone inherits, and sometimes the magic just springs up from nowhere. But... you likely did, yes."

It wasn't a straight answer, any more than any of the other answers had been, but it was something to try and cling to as Bailey's world changed. It was best to find the positive. This was something her mother had given her, like a heirloom. Whether it was the truth or not, she tried not to worry about. What mattered was that it made her feel a little better.

That was more or less how they left it. The walk, and the revelation, and the burden of realization had all sapped Bailey's strength and although Chloe really wanted her to come in and speak with Aria and Frances, she couldn't seem to convince herself to do so. Chloe hugged her, promised it would be alright, and then let her walk home.

Ryan was up when she arrived, pecking away on a laptop, his aged eyes squinting at the screen over his spectacles. He barely noticed when Bailey came in until she hugged him from behind. "I love you, Dad," she muttered into his shoulder.

Her father touched her arms, and leaned his head into hers, chuckling. "Well I appreciate it, Red. I love you, too. You out running around with Ave and Pip?" When they were little, he'd called them his three chipmunks, always getting in and out of trouble together.

"Yeah," she lied, and felt awful for it. She wanted to tell him the truth but… there was no telling what he might think of it all.

She had to concentrate perpetually to keep from reading his thoughts, and there was still a dull, distant whisper of them in the back of her mind. It seemed wrong. Reading the thoughts of a murderer to bring him or her to justice was a gift. Inadvertently violating the privacy of those around her, her friends and family that she loved and trusted to simply tell her what they thought—that was a burden. A heavy one that she wasn't sure she could handle.

She climbed the stairs to her room, and opened her window to listen to the ocean for a while to think things over. All of this seemed too good to be real, which meant that it probably was; while at the same time laying something thick and smothering over her that felt all too real. It was difficult not to feel somehow trapped by it all. Dueling urges took over her thoughts—the urge to dive headlong into a new world, and the urge to tiptoe carefully around it and quickly make a break before it got its hooks in her and refused to let go.

Funny. She'd often dreamed about this very thing as a girl. Now that it was here, impossibly, she wasn't sure she wanted it to be real anymore. It was this thought of concern that carried her to sleep, slowly congealing into a decision just before she drifted off.

Tomorrow, Bailey would leave Coven Grove.

Wendy had always said that people don't make good decisions when they were stressed. "Never make rash decisions," she said, "always sleep on it, especially when you feel pressed—a good night's sleep often clarifies things just enough to know what you need to do."

Bailey had done that. In the morning, the whole event with Chloe seemed somewhat more distant, less threatening. Still, she came to the same conclusion. Already her head was pounding, and keeping them from getting too loud was like balancing a tea cup on her head while she showered, and brushed her teeth, and dressed, and by the time she descended the stairs to have breakfast with Ryan she was already frazzled and she hadn't even been awake for an hour. Her dreams had been nonsensical and disturbing, and she didn't feel rested.

She couldn't live like this. And she couldn't shake the sense of impending doom that seemed inexorably attached to being a witch. It felt dangerous, and somehow wrong; like she was breaking a law somewhere and that soon someone would come for her. Maybe they already had come for Martha, after all.

It took all of the morning for her to work up the nerve to tell her father, and by then Avery was with them in the library. Eager for another crack at the mystery, Piper showed up just before lunch, dressed somewhat more for walking and chomping at the bit to find out what Avery had discovered. She apparently had some fascinating bits of history about the town and the murders that had happened in the earlier part of the twentieth century.

All the tension, the need to gossip and discuss and to keep playing this silly game of Private Eye, only served to make Bailey more and more nervous and stressed until, finally, she made the announcement. It had no preamble, no lead-in, and no context.

"I'm leaving," she announced, standing at the end of the table where Piper, Avery, and Ryan were gathered to eat lunch and discuss theories.

All three faces turned on her, silent and confused.

"Okay," Piper said slowly. "Where to?" It was

obvious she was thinking maybe somewhere in town, or the bathroom. Bailey slumped forward, leaning heavily on one of the worn wooden chairs around the library table. "I mean that I'm leaving Coven Grove," she said, watching the table instead of their eyes in order to maintain her nerve.

After a heartbeat of shocked silence, Avery and Piper began speaking at once. Ryan was conspicuously silent.

"You can't leave in the middle of this," Avery said, eyes wide.

"What are you thinking, Bee? You can't just leave!" Piper cried.

Bailey raised a hand for silence. She addressed Avery first. "This whole... murder—it's not something we can help with. We should leave it to the Sheriff's department. It's dangerous, for one thing. You think whoever killed Martha Tells won't think twice about killing one of us if we go poking around where we don't belong?"

She looked at Piper, and wished that it was her business to simply tell her friend that she knew everything wasn't 'alright' at home and that she desperately wanted to be there for her friend but... Piper's jaw was already set, the beginning of her process of convincing herself and everyone else that she was fine with it. "I'll stay in touch," Bailey said to her. "I'll even come back and visit. There are just... things out there that I need to find for myself. Answers. And... other things I don't know what they are yet."

Piper understood. "It's got to do with your mother, right? Not Wendy, I mean but your birth mother."

Avery clenched his jaw, and exhaled sharply but didn't say anything.

"Some of it," Bailey admitted. "Yes." It would be so much easier if she could just tell them…

"I understand," Ryan said. He looked older, suddenly, and more tired than he usually was. He took his spectacles off and set them down on the table, and then rubbed his eyes briefly. "You've been here your whole life, and it's been comfortable but all this," he waved at the papers and books on the table, and the situation at large, "it has you wondering what else is out there, what else you don't know. I get it. I'd say you got it from me, but—"

Bailey sighed, and rounded the table to hug her father. "Of course I got it from you," she muttered.

Ryan hugged her back until she let him go, and then pursed his lips. "Your mother never told me who you were born to," he said after a moment. "But… if you're going to go looking for her, maybe you could start with Wendy's old files. They're in the basement here. You can take them with you. I don't know if there are any answers there, she was tight lipped about everything that needed it, but maybe there are enough pieces for you to follow. I understand needing to see other places, ask new questions, and get answers." He looked around the table at Avery and Piper before he settled on Bailey again. "Maybe better than most."

It was just enough of a reprimand that her two friends crumpled a little under the weight of it.

Bailey did understand. It was sudden. It had to be. If she spent too long thinking about it, she'd change her mind.

"Are you sure about this?" Avery asked. "I mean… why all of a sudden? Did something happen? I feel like I'm missing pieces here."

He was, of course. That was Avery's intuition; his gut wasn't often wrong about things. This time, though, Bailey had to hope he'd at least doubt himself a little. "Someone was killed," she said. "Isn't that enough? The tours are going to shut down, and I love the library but I can't stay sequestered in it forever."

"Then go," Piper sighed. But she managed to summon up a weak smile. "There are definitely times I wished I had gotten out while I had the chance. Even for a little while."

Avery was the only one unwilling to concede. "Bailey… Bee… you know I want what's best for you. But… I can't shake this feeling that you're supposed to be here. That whatever you're looking for is here, in Coven Grove. Just like whoever killed Martha and—"

"Ave," Piper hissed.

He bit off whatever else he was going to say and looked momentarily ashamed of whatever card he was about to play.

"I guess… I'll just miss you. God, this town is so white bread already; how will I survive without my Bee? No one else understands me like you do." He looked genuinely devastated.

Maybe, Bailey thought… maybe Avery could come with her. She could tell him everything, Chloe and her paranoia be damned. Avery would understand, wouldn't he?

But… what if he didn't? What if he was constantly worried that Bailey was in his head, reading his thoughts? What if he was just terrified of the supernatural once he was confronted with it? There was just no way to know. After all, Bailey was the one who was supposedly a witch, and she was already terrified of the implications. Bailey pulled him from his chair to embrace him. "I promise I'll come back for you," she whispered. God, just hours before she'd been absolutely sure she needed to do this. She'd known it would be painful, but the reality was something else entirely.

They could have claimed that she had an obligation to stay here. They could have told her that they'd been the ones to get her through Wendy's death, the ones whose shoulders she'd cried on, the people who had put her almost back together after it happened. And if they had, it would have convinced her that she had to stay.

They didn't, though, because they were her friends. That was almost somehow worse.

Avery let her go. Bailey heard his thoughts when he did. It was an accident, and she pulled away from them like they had burned her, instantly ashamed of having listened even inadvertently.

"Whatever she's hiding, she'll tell me when she's ready."

Bailey wanted to cry. There was nothing but warm, compassionate worry and hope on his mind, tinged with a little bit of the sting of it all.

She was so stricken by it that she pulled him close again, and whispered to him, "I promise I'll tell you everything one day."

He nodded, unsurprised—they just knew each other that well, she supposed—and then let her go to stuff his hands in his pockets. "So… in case the tour business doesn't shut down, I guess I'll probably take over… maybe you should drop off all your junk at the tour office before you go. I could probably figure out some way to make it all work. Especially if Poppy isn't coming back."

Bailey frowned. "She isn't back yet?"

"Not as far as anyone can tell," Piper said.

Ryan sighed, and put his glasses back on. "You know she doesn't deal with crisis very well, but the Sheriff's department says they consider it highly suspicious. Who knows."

Bailey felt herself being tugged back into it, and gently pulled herself away from it all before she fell headlong into this town's problems and got herself into even more trouble. "Well, they'll sort it out. You three need to keep your distance from it, okay?"

"What does she know, I wonder?" It was hard to say whose thought it was, but she knew it was a thought that wasn't her own, now that she knew what to look for. It had the kind of patient, watchful quality she associated with Ryan, though. Maybe that was the key to knowing who was thinking at you. Either way, she focused her attention on her own thoughts, her own senses. Ryan's mind was none of her business. "Well... I don't want a long goodbye. I'll run a few things to the tour office, and I guess just leave you my keys," she said to Avery. "So I'll be back in a bit." She backed away, and then turned and found the basement door.

She did find Wendy's old files, though only because she understood Ryan's arcane system of organization. She also found the few boxes of odds and ends, souvenir projects for the Caves that were half finished in some of the boxes, and completed in the others but never put on display. Maybe Avery could pass them off as his own to get into Poppy's good graces when she came back. Maybe they would even help make the most of whatever Tourists didn't see the headlines about the murder.

Eventually, Avery helped her. He was quiet, and didn't bug her about her choice as they worked. When the last box was in the car, he hugged her again. "Just come back, okay? When you find whatever you're looking for. Don't leave me alone here. I know it's selfish but... I need you, Bee. Like... to survive here."

"You should leave this town, too, Avery," She told

him. "When you're ready."

He shrugged. "Well… I know. But that's not yet, so…" His eyes cast about, and finally settled on her again. "Bye, Bailey. I love you. Just… take care of yourself. And call me. A lot."

She smiled as he left her, and tried to stamp down the questions that plagued her. Be strong. Do this. Get out of this town, away from this, and at least get some perspective. Then, decide if you want to come back.

Her resolved properly renewed, she started to get into her car.

"Leaving?" Chloe called from a few yards away. She had a box, and was headed toward Bailey.

Bailey wondered if she'd been reading her mind. It seemed unfair. She tried to focus her attention on Chloe, but the woman raised an eyebrow up as she leaned on the car door. She handed Bailey the box, heavy with cupcakes. "You can't read me unless I want you to," she said. "Same goes with the others. Witching one-oh-one. Which you'll know soon, if you stick around but…" she looked at the back seat full of boxes, "…something tells me you aren't."

Every minute she spent with the woman was one she wasn't on the road, and one more opportunity for Chloe to change her mind. The worst of it was that Bailey honestly wasn't sure she could be certain, if she did change it, that it was her own intention. After all, if someone could read minds, what else could they do?

Still, she felt like she owed her friend at least the time of day. "Hop in," she said. "I'm stopping by the tour office first. We can talk on the way there, but my mind is made up."

Chloe gave her a long look, and then nodded. She came around and slipped into the passenger seat.

The tour office wasn't far, driving. They didn't have much time to talk. So Chloe made the most of it, not bothering to mince words about why Bailey wanted to leave. Maybe she already knew.

"Your place is here," she said simply, "with us. We can teach you about your ability, and about so much more. What you're experiencing now is just the tip of an iceberg that runs deep, Bailey. You need to know about yourself."

"This part of it is bad enough," Bailey said, eyes glued to the road. "I don't want to keep secrets from my friends, either, and even just what you said—that my place is here—it feels like I don't have a choice in the matter. What about what I want?"

"What do you want, then?" Chloe asked.

"I want to run my own life," Bailey said. "I want to find my own answers, and I want to know about my mother, and who she is, and where she is and if she's still alive and why she gave me up and…" She had to stop, struggling against a knot in her throat.

"I suppose I understand all of that," Chloe said quietly. "I didn't have much of a choice myself, a lot of the time… I get it. But what we have, Bailey; it's precious in a way you haven't had time to comprehend yet. It's new, and scary, and if you're anything like I was you're worried about what it all means. And I promise, it does mean something—something beautiful, Bailey. There's nothing to be afraid of except being alone. And you aren't, my love. You're not alone in this. I promise."

Bailey felt something unsaid. She glanced at Chloe. A moment later it came.

"And if you want to find your mother… this gift could be your one connection to her," Chloe said. She said it gently, knowing that hearing it would be painful. It was. Bailey wanted to scream at her for playing that card. It wasn't fair.

"If I learn," Bailey asked, trying not to sound bitter about it, "can this… gift help me find her?"

"I don't know, sweetheart," Chloe said. "But if it can… do you really want to give it up?"

They pulled into the tour office parking lot and Bailey, ran her fingers through her hair. Chloe had a point. Of course she had a point. But she wished she didn't. "That's a decision I can't make here," she said. "I need to be away from all of this to think about it." She opened her door. "I need to take all this inside."

"I'll help you," Chloe said.

Bailey wanted distance from the woman. She wanted to think things through on her own. "I can handle it, it's just a couple of boxes."

Chloe fixed her with a look that brooked no arguments. "There's a killer on the loose somewhere. You really think I'm going to let you walk around out here alone? No. I'll help you, and then I'll let you go on your way."

Bailey only sighed, and nodded. It was a fair point.

And, as they came to the door of the building and Bailey unlocked it, she nearly dropped the box she'd propped on her knee to get the lock. Maybe Chloe had been right to come after all—someone was already inside.

Chapter 11

"Do you hear that?" Bailey whispered.

Chloe pressed close to the door, and shook her head. "No, what?"

Bailey shook her head, and tapped her skull. "I mean… you know."

Chloe's eyes grew distant. A moment later she frowned. "Is that… Poppy?"

Bailey would know the odd, frantic cadence of Poppy's thoughts anywhere; they were exactly like her words, and they were rife with the same acerbic, permanently irritated sting. It hurt to hear them. It was no wonder Bailey always got a headache around the woman.

"I was in the kitchen, and then the bathroom, and then my bedroom, and I went back to the sink in the kitchen, and then the office… where did I leave them?"

Chloe and Bailey shared a look, but Bailey shrugged. It wasn't uncommon for Poppy to lose things. They pushed quietly through the door, and Chloe took Bailey's silent cue to stay quiet. The last thing Bailey wanted was to have to have this conversation about her leaving with Poppy. Her boss would lose her mind, and scream until she was hoarse about how Bailey was abandoning her, letting her down, and whatever else came to her mind to shout about.

Funny thing, though… the lights weren't on inside the place.

If Poppy had lost something, it seemed like she'd have turned the lights on so she could find it. Probably lipstick, or her keys—or her check book. She lost that a lot, though not nearly often enough and normally only when it came time to write Bailey a check…

Bailey had pushed the woman's thoughts out of her head—something about the need she felt to have Poppy far away seemed to help. But as she and Chloe padded into the front office to drop off Bailey's boxes, Chloe froze in the doorway. She nearly dropped her box, and Bailey had to move fast to help her steady it.

When she met Chloe's eyes, her blood chilled. "What?" She mouthed.

Chloe looked toward the back of the house, and Bailey did as well. She reached for Poppy's broadcasting mind as she looked, and found it easily, banging up against her own thoughts like an angry wasp trying to get through a window. She winced, learning very quickly that some people's minds actually tasted bad, somehow, on whatever psychic equivalent of a tongue she had going on up there in her head.

All of that faded, though, when she felt and heard Poppy's panicked hunt continue. "Should have gotten rid of the thing right away," Poppy was screaming at herself mentally, her thoughts crisp and sharp. "I could be out of the country by now. Damn that woman, still trying to ruin me even in death…" It wasn't completely clear what she was looking for, but the intention behind it was.

She was mortally terrified, angry, and looking for something that scared her to death.

Chloe hadn't waited for Bailey to say anything. Instead, she had already picked up the phone and was dialing. A second later, she ducked behind the desk to whisper quietly into the cordless. Bailey couldn't hear her, but she had to have been calling the Sheriff's department.

Poppy was coming toward them now, retracing steps mentally, trying to find keys. Keys to the safe, Bailey imagined. Normally they were in the center drawer of the office… she crept across the room, and pulled the drawer out silently. There was lipstick in front which meant Poppy had probably been digging and… there they were, toward the back. Bailey started to grasp them and then stopped. Better not put her fingerprints on them. She'd just heard Poppy name what she was looking for.

She caught Chloe's eye across the darkened room. Chloe had heard it too.

A rock. Poppy was looking for a 'stupid rock' that was all she needed to get rid of. She'd put it in the safe and then misplaced the keys, and was thinking that instead she should have just hurled the thing into the ocean over the cliffs. She'd panicked, though, and was someone here? Whose car was that…

Bailey was so caught up listening and trying to follow Poppy's rapid, panic filled thoughts that she didn't even realize until the office light clicked on that she'd reached them.

She stared at Bailey, standing behind the desk, and then spotted Chloe squatting behind the far end.

Instantly, she lost her mind, and Bailey even flinched as hot, red, nearly murderous rage filled Poppy's mind and seemed like it might burn Bailey right where she stood. "What the hell are you doing here? Get out! Out! Both of you! I'll call the cops!"

"I have a key," Bailey snapped. "I came to drop off…" what had she come for? "…boxes. Things, for the office; for the tours!" It was disorienting, extricating herself so suddenly from Poppy's mind. "They know," Poppy thought. "They know. They're in here in the dark, looking for it. No, no,no, no, no…"

"Poppy, calm down," Bailey urged. She walked slowly from behind the desk, her hands up, fingers spread for peace—though she knew it was likely useless.

"Don't talk to me about calming down," Poppy screamed. "Office hours are over and you… you don't belong here unless there are tours or… just go! Get out! You're fired! You hear me? Give me back my key! Now!" Her face was twisted with anger that made her suddenly hideous. She'd genuinely lost her mind— Bailey could barely make out any of the seemingly random things that were broadcasting from it, it was all mixed up and backwards and senseless. A picture that had been broken and then pieced back together incompletely. Most of it meaningless but some of it—images and fragments of thoughts—stood out in stark, still relief against the rest.

Poppy was worried about a warrant. That's why she had parked almost outside town, near the beach, and come up the long way. So no one would see her. They couldn't serve a warrant if they couldn't find her, she thought. She needed to come in and get rid of the evidence. The rock. It was the only thing that would tie her to the scene.

"The safe," Chloe said, standing from behind the end of the desk. She laid the phone on the top of it, face down. "It's in the safe, isn't it, Poppy?"

"What are you talking about?" Poppy barked. "You don't even work here. Martha warned me about you; that you'd come sneaking around. You probably killed her, didn't you?"

"You know that isn't true, Poppy," Bailey said quietly. "You killed Martha, didn't you." It wasn't a question.

"How dare you accuse me of…! You awful horrible little skank! I saw you with Trevor, flirting and flouncing—you two probably offed her together!" She sneered, jabbing a finger with a broken nail at Bailey. "Yeah, right! He hated her, and so did you I could see it on your face from the moment I told you she was in town. I even remember thinking that maybe it was a bad idea to put you two together; I've always thought you were unstable! I should have known, I should have known!"

Her thoughts told a different story, though. One that Bailey heard clearly. "No," she said calmly, though her heart was pounding in her chest. "You killed Martha, Poppy. She... fell? But she got up again... not then..."

"After," Chloe provided. She was staring intently at Poppy, taking slow steps toward her. "It was after. You came back and heard her talking to someone... no, on her phone. About what, Poppy? What was she saying that made you so angry?"

Poppy had stopped speaking actual words. She was sputtering and staggering backward a bit, her eyes wide and rolling. "No, no... you can't know..."

Bailey caught more pieces as Poppy's mind rehashed the scene again, and again. "She was going to sue?" She frowned. "She didn't look injured."

"She didn't look injured to Poppy," Chloe corrected. "It's all from her twisted filter."

That put so much else into perspective that the rest of the story seemed to coalesce around that thought, and Bailey felt it come tumbling into her mind even as Poppy began to try and talk herself out of remembering it again.

Martha had fallen, and Poppy attempted to help her up. It had made her dress dirty, but there was some soda water in a cooler, and Poppy, ever the sycophant, had offered to get it right away and fix the spot up right as rain. When she came back, she'd heard Martha on the phone.

"How injured do I have to be?" The memory of Martha's voice was distorted in Poppy's mind, echoing wrong, the same words booming in Bailey's head as she heard them. "Legally, I mean. You tell me, and I'll take a dive right now… no, of course you didn't hear me say that, darling. Well I don't know if they have insurance, but they have money; this woman lives half her life in Vegas and Baja, or some place. She won't stop going on about it, it's driving me insane. Just call me back then, and let me know. ACT pays crap. I bet we could sue this place for at least a couple million. Well then I'll make sure it counts, Seymour."

The rest of it was a red blur, almost. Poppy had come enraged. How dare this woman threaten to sue her? Sue her! For a little trip over her own too-long dress that she couldn't even afford to have tailored properly. It didn't matter what she planned to 'reveal' about the 'secret' of the Caves. Poppy would be ruined. All her money, dried up. She'd be stuck here in this crappy little back-woods town forever.

So she'd done what seemed, at the time, like the only course of action. She had charged Martha with a large rock the moment she hung up her phone. Bailey actually physically squeezed her eyes shut to avoid seeing the next part, but there was no avoiding it now.

After, Poppy had taken the phone, and the rock, and brought them both up to the office. Dazed, confused, and panicked, she put them both in the safe. She pulled open the top drawer, and pulled a flask out, and drained it and tried to decide what to do next. Unable to think clearly, she'd simply left town.

All of it happened in seconds. Bailey simply gasped when it hit her, and sat against the edge of the desk. Chloe, however, was howling with rage.

"You killed our sister!" She screamed. The air felt thick, and hot, and moist. "Over money? Because you wanted to hold on to your worthless, meager fortune?" There were tears streaming down her face.

"I… I couldn't… you can't possibly…" Poppy sputtered a moment more, and then fell to her knees, her face a mess of tears and smeared eyeliner. "She would have ruined me… forever. This is all I have and she wanted to take it from me because she was a greedy, selfish…" she shook her head, and put her face in her hands, and sobbed.

"Did you hear?" Chloe asked. Bailey looked up. Chloe had the phone to her ear again. She looked calmer, resolved; but merciless.

Bailey couldn't blame her. She stood from the desk, and stared down at Poppy's pitiful, wretched form crumpled on the floor in her expensive skirt and blouse. "I never thought you were capable of something so terrible, Poppy," she whispered.

Poppy's eyes were red, and puffy, and furious when she looked up. Bailey thought, for a moment, she might attack. Instead, though, she just stared. "You couldn't have known unless…" she swallowed, and her eyebrows knit together in disbelief. "It's true, isn't it? What Martha said. I heard her once, whispering to someone on the phone. About the Caves. About… witches."

Bailey's eyes widened, and Poppy barked a sharp laugh of triumph, like she'd caught her in a lie. "I knew it!"

"Don't listen to her," Chloe said. "Poppy's lost her mind. She couldn't take the guilt of what she'd done. She's projecting." She sighed, sad and disappointed. "It's textbook."

Bailey turned to stare at Chloe, who didn't seem at all concerned about the fact that Poppy had just named them witches. Of course; they'd read her mind. It had to be obvious, didn't it?

But Chloe only shook her head slightly, maybe hearing Bailey's thoughts.

So Bailey kept her mouth shut, her jaw clenched tight, and she and Chloe stayed there and watched Poppy until Sheriff Larson arrived to arrest her. Bailey showed him where the keys to the safe were. Inside, just like Bailey had seen in Poppy's mind, was a rust-stained rock and a cell phone with the battery removed. Poor Martha hadn't even been able to afford a smart phone. Justice was done. They'd caught the bad guy. And Bailey had her strange new gift to thank for it. Hooray, right?

Somehow, though, it didn't feel like cause for celebration.

Epilogue

Bailey was, of course, detained for questioning. She hated having to lie, but understood that she couldn't claim to have read Poppy's mind. Instead, she followed with Chloe's story. Poppy had been driven mad by guilt. She'd found Bailey and Chloe dropping off souvenirs that Bailey had made for the tour business to sell—that part held up, of course, because that was exactly what they'd been doing. So, the rest did as well.

Plus, the Sheriff's department had heard Poppy's confession at the end. The story that quickly circulated was that Bailey and Chloe had somehow deduced much of what happened, and confronted Poppy with it and she'd cracked. They were briefly celebrated as heroes of the town. Sheriff Larson even offered to make them honorary deputies. Both Bailey and Chloe declined, and kept their heads down about all of it. It was possibly a joke anyway.

Avery, however, was beside himself. "I can't believe you went and caught the killer by yourself!" He wailed when she saw him later, at the bakery.

Piper was less surprised. "I knew the whole leaving town thing was just a ruse. You never could keep your nose out of a good mystery."

"I wish you'd taken us," Avery complained.

Bailey sighed. "It wasn't the plan. We were just in the right place at the right time."

No one quite seemed to believe that. Including Chloe. She was convinced that it was all tied together; that they'd been merely instruments of higher powers, who had wanted to serve justice to Martha's killer. While Bailey wasn't sure about that she had to admit… it all seemed strangely ordered.

"So, are you still leaving?" Avery asked.

That was possibly the worst part of the fall out—and also, Chloe claimed, part of some mysterious, mystical plan as well—Bailey was expected to testify. She was not leaving town any time soon.

"Is it okay that I don't hate that for you very much?" Avery mused.

"Yeah," Piper said. "I'm glad you're sticking around, at least for a little while longer."

Bailey dreaded it. Already, the two of them were constantly peering and watching—or at any rate it felt that way—and she hated having a secret from them. Still, she smiled and touched Piper's hand, and smiled. "Me too."

Gradually, the commotion died down. As much as it was going to, anyway. Gloria and Trevor stuck around, each claiming to be charmed by the quaintness of Coven Grove, although Bailey knew that what really had them interested was what Martha had never had the chance to tell them her secret about the Caves.

She took that concern to Chloe, but the older woman only shared a knowing look with Aria and Frances. "The Caves have a way of keeping their secrets to themselves," Chloe explained.

"They don't really care for outsiders," Aria added.

"Those two are just two in a long line of curious interlopers," Frances finished.

Bailey wasn't certain of that. Gloria especially had a kind of wide-eyed zeal when she talked about the Caves, and about Martha. And Trevor continued to be polite and charming, but Bailey knew his interest was as keen as Gloria's; he was just better at hiding it.

Poppy's hearing set her on course for a trial. Bailey and Chloe both testified, and half the town packed into the courtroom galley to observe. The local news treated it almost like a red carpet event. Lost was the real memory of Martha Tells, it seemed, except to those that knew her and called her sister. In its place was the iconic image of a woman who was always almost famous but never quite made it. In a way, it was even more sad than the truth, and Bailey grew angry over the media's focus on the insane Poppy Winters, who ranted about witches and magic caves, but was ultimately ruled sane and received a sentence of twenty five years.

And then, just like that, it was over. Justice had been served, the world moved on.

Bailey was once again ready to consider leaving town.

But there was one thing that, Chloe insisted, she had to

undergo first. If, at that point, she decided she was going to leave, then she could and no one would try to talk her out of it.

It was, Bailey learned, her official initiation.

"The first initiation," Chloe explained, "is like an introduction. You can still walk away at that point, if you want to. Well… you can always walk away, but there is no geas associated with the first cave."

It was a word Bailey didn't know. "Geesh?" She asked. "Like birds?"

Chloe tittered. "No, not a bird. A geas is like a promise, but rooted in magic. The deeper you go into the mystery of our tradition, the more important the secrets you learn become." She waved at Aria and Frances, who sat elsewhere in the wide attic above the bakery. Aria was knitting casually, while Frances appeared to be making some kind of doll out of an assortment of materials arrayed before her. Corn husk was among them; the rest Bailey couldn't tell from a distance.

"But not for the first one?" She asked.

Chloe nodded, and assured her there was no risk at all.

Bailey believed her, because she was making an effort to trust the women despite their cryptic words and tendency to obfuscate even the simplest answers behind riddles and parables. "Alright. Then… I suppose I can stay another few days."

A few days became a week—the night of the next full moon. Bailey began to believe that the last weeks had all been some elaborate ploy to simply delay her leaving until she had no choice.

But the night did come, and she went with Chloe and Aria and Frances to the entrance of the caves just as the full moon rose to its apex in the starry, clear sky. There, she changed into a simple linen robe and the women anointed her arms, and feet, and eyes, and temples with fragrant oils as they chanted and sang and called out to what they called the 'genius loci' of the caves—the elemental spirit of the place itself, a sort of primal intelligence that suffused the place.

When they were done, they ushered Bailey excitedly into the place, where she stood in the center of the first great cavern. Each of the women with her went to a different part of it, and together they raised their voice in a somber, haunting sort of song that seemed to bounce around the odd angles of the caves walls, blending together until the acoustics made it seem almost as if the cave itself were singing.

She watched the writing and the pictographs, just as she'd been instructed, patiently enduring the strange ritual and alert to any subtle changes in herself that she might miss. What she was supposed to experience was a mystery. The women weren't able to tell her because, they said, it was different for everyone.

But, as Bailey listened to the rolling chant that seemed to so closely match the rhythm and call of the ocean after a time, she did notice something. Her eyes went wide as she saw it happening. In an instant, she realized that she couldn't possibly leave Coven Grove. Not now. Not after this.

A smile crept onto Bailey's lips as, finally, it all began to make sense. Of course she could never translate the nonsense words. They really were just mixed up letters. But not anymore. Before her eyes, the paintings on the cave wall *moved*.

*****

Thanks for reading! I hope you enjoyed the book and it would mean so much to me if you could leave a review. Reviews help authors gain more exposure and keep us writing your favorite stories.

You can find all of my books by visiting my Author Page.

Sign up for Constance Barker's New Releases Newsletter where you can find out when my next book is coming out and for special discounted pricing.

I never share or sell your email.

Visit me on Facebook and give me feedback on the characters and their stories.

Old School Diner Cozy Mysteries

Murder at Stake

Murder Well Done

A Side Order of Deception

The Curiosity Shop Cozy Mysteries

The Curious Case of the Cursed Spectacles

The Curious Case of the Cursed Dice

The Curious Case of the Cursed Dagger

The We're Not Dead Yet Club

Fetch a Pail of Murder

Wedding Bells and Death Knells

Murder or Bust

Pinched, Pilfered and a Pitchfork

A Hot Spot of Murder

Witchy Women of Coven Grove Series

The Witching on the Wall

A Witching Well of Magic

Witching the Night Away

Witching There's Another Way

Witching Your Life Away

Witching You Wouldn't Go

Witching for a Miracle

Teasen & Pleasen Hair Salon Series

A Hair Raising Blowout

Wash, Rinse, Die

Holiday Hooligans

Color Me Dead

False Nails & Tall Tales

Caesar's Creek Series

A Frozen Scoop of Murder (Caesars Creek Mystery Series Book One)

Death by Chocolate Sundae (Caesars Creek Mystery Series Book Two)

Soft Serve Secrets (Caesars Creek Mystery Series Book Three)

Ice Cream You Scream (Caesars Creek Mystery Series Book Four)

Double Dip Dilemma (Caesars Creek Mystery Series Book Five)

Melted Memories (Caesars Creek Mystery Series Book Six)

Triple Dip Debacle(Caesars Creek Mystery Series Book Seven)

Whipped Wedding Woes(Caesars Creek Mystery Series Book Eight)

A Sprinkle of Tropical Trouble(Caesars Creek Mystery Series Book Nine)

A Drizzle of Deception(Caesars Creek Mystery Series Book Ten)

Sweet Home Mystery Series

Creamed at the Coffee Cabana (Sweet Home Mystery Series Book One)

A Caffeinated Crunch (Sweet Home Mystery Series Book Two)

A Frothy Fiasco (Sweet Home Mystery Series Book Three)

Punked by the Pumpkin(Sweet Home Mystery Series Book Four)

Peppermint Pandemonium(Sweet Home Mystery Series Book Five)

Expresso Messo(Sweet Home Mystery Series Book Six)

A Cuppa Cruise Conundrum(Sweet Home Mystery Series Book Seven)

The Brewing Bride(Sweet Home Mystery Series Book Eight)

Whispering Pines Mystery Series

A Sinister Slice of Murder

Sanctum of Shadows (Whispering Pines Mystery Series)

Curse of the Bloodstone Arrow (Whispering Pines Mystery Series)

Fright Night at the Haunted Inn (Whispering Pines Mystery Series)

Mad River Mystery Series

A Wicked Whack

A Prickly Predicament

A Malevolent Menace

Made in United States
North Haven, CT
03 June 2024

53274205R00078